W9-BSQ-547

Dawn's Family Feud
Ann M. Martin

AN
APPLE
PAPERBACK

SCHOLASTIC INC.
New York Toronto London Auckland Sydney

Cover art by Hodges Soileau

No part of this publication may be reproduced in whole or in part, or stored in a retrieval system, or transmitted in any form or by any means, electronic, mechanical, photocopying, recording, or otherwise, without written permission of the publisher. For information regarding permission, write to Scholastic Inc., 730 Broadway, New York, NY 10003.

ISBN 0-590-45666-0

12 11 10 9 8 7 6 5 4 3 2 1   3 4 5 6 7 8/9

Printed in the U.S.A.   40

First Scholastic printing, May 1993

The author gratefully acknowledges
Jahnna Beecham
and
Malcolm Hillgartner
for their help in
preparing this manuscript.

Dawn's Family Feud

CHAPTER 1

"Dawn, honey?"

Mom's voice was coming from upstairs. "Could you bring me a bottle of that squirty stuff?"

"Squirty stuff?" I repeated. "You mean, like catsup?"

"No. It's not for eating. It's for cleaning the bathroom. You spray it on things and the dirt is supposed to just disappear."

"Oh!" I giggled. "*That* squirty stuff." I moved to the bottom of the stairs and shouted up, "The Wipe Away tile cleaner is under the bathroom sink."

"There it is!" Mom shouted. "Silly me. It was there all the time and I never even noticed it."

I hate to say it, but my mom is basically a slob. She usually hates housecleaning, but this Saturday was different. She was actually happy to scrub the bathroom floor. You see, we were all getting ready for my brother Jeff's visit.

I'm Dawn Schafer. I'm thirteen and I live in Connecticut with my mom. Jeff, who is ten, lives in California with my dad. You've probably guessed that my parents are divorced. When the split happened, Mom brought Jeff and me back to the town of Stoneybrook, where she grew up. It was rough on all of us. Lucky for me, I met Mary Anne Spier and we liked each other instantly. Then Mary Anne introduced me to the members of the Baby-sitters Club (I'll tell you more about them later) and soon I had lots of friends. But Jeff was always getting in fights with this kid named Jerry Haney, and doing badly in school. He really hated being here. That's why Mom decided he would be happier if he went back to California and lived with Dad. Jeff *is* much happier now, but I miss him. And my old home. You see, I'm a California girl at heart.

In case you're wondering, I have long hair (almost to my waist), that's pale blonde, and blue eyes that some people say are the color of the ocean. I like sunshine and healthy food like carrot sticks and granola. I wear clothes that are comfortable. And I am very independent.

Back to Mary Anne. She's my best friend. And guess what? Now she's also my stepsister! Her dad (Richard) married my mom (Sharon). This is how it happened. Mary Anne and I discovered that our parents had dated in high school. We found all this romantic stuff they'd written to each other in their senior yearbooks. So we decided to try to get them back together. You see, Mr. Spier's wife died when Mary Anne was little. After that he became this stern lonely guy who was really strict with Mary Anne. (He used to make her wear little kid dresses and fix her hair in pigtails.) Mom's divorce was hard and she was lonely, too. Anyway, it was the perfect time for them to meet. They started dating and fell in love all over again. Isn't that cool? And then they decided to get married and now Mom is Mrs. Spier.

We all live in this creaky old farmhouse that's nearly two hundred years old. It was built in 1795 and it even has a secret passage that might be haunted. The passage leads from the barn to my room. I found out that during the Civil War it was used as a hiding place for the Underground Railroad. Isn't that neat?

I really like my new family, but I have to say that there's been a hole inside of me ever since Jeff went back to California. It was hard enough living without Dad but when my brother left, it took me a long time to get over it.

"Jeff's coming in six days!" I announced as Mary Anne and I cleaned his room. "He'll be here for one whole week. I can't wait."

"Have you figured out what you're going to do with him?" Mary Anne asked.

"A zillion things," I said, smoothing out the sheet on his twin bed. "Play Frisbee in the park, go bike riding, play some video games. Jeff loves video games. Oh, and I want to take him to that new toy store downtown."

"That's a lot to do in such a short time," Mary Anne said as she dusted the desk. "It's too bad we have to go to school while Jeff's here."

"You're right," I said with a sigh. "Oh, well. It's only for Monday, Tuesday, and Wednesday. Then we have that four day weekend."

"Dad wants us to take a family trip," Mary Anne added. "To Washington D.C. or Boston."

"Either one would be fun," I said.

Just then, Richard stuck his head in the door. "How's the cleaning coming?"

Mary Anne waved her dust rag. "It's going great, Dad. We've vacuumed under the bed and in the closet. I've checked all the dresser drawers for dust and Dawn is just finishing making the bed."

Richard raised one eyebrow and peered over his glasses at the room. I held my breath, waiting for him to spot some speck of dirt.

You see, Richard and my mom are practically exact opposites. She's kind of messy and really absentminded. I'm always finding hedge clippers in the bread drawer or her high heels in the refrigerator or the TV remote control in the bathroom cabinet. Richard, on the other hand, is Mr. Organized. He arranges his books alphabetically and color codes his socks. He's a clean fiend and likes dishes and counters to shine.

"Make sure those sheets have hospital corners," Richard said, pointing to the bed. "We want everything shipshape for Jeff."

"Hospital corners?" I had no idea what he was talking about.

Richard untucked the top sheet that I had just spent five minutes smoothing out. "Here, I'll show you. It's the most efficient way to make a bed. Hospitals developed this technique because they change sheets more often than any other institution." I watched as he tucked a corner under the bed, making sure he had a straight crease on the remaining part, and then folded that under the mattress. The corner of the sheet looked like the back of an envelope.

"There!" He stepped back and surveyed his work proudly. "What do you think?"

I didn't want to tell him that I thought my

way had looked just as nice so I said, "It looks really neat and tidy."

Richard smiled and nodded. "That's good. Jeff will appreciate that, I'm sure."

I was sure Jeff wouldn't even notice. You see, Jeff is like Mom and me — pretty relaxed about things. Making the bed to him means throwing a bedspread over a wrinkled sheet and tossing the pillow on top. But I didn't mention that.

Richard clapped his hands together. "I'm looking forward to this visit with Jeff. It'll really give us a chance to get to know each other. Yes indeed. Yes indeed."

Richard seemed a little nervous. I could tell because he kept repeating himself. But I also knew why. Mom wasn't able to take time off from her job and Mary Anne and I were going to be in school for the first three days of the week so Richard was going to have to take time off from *his* job and look after Jeff all by himself. I had heard Mom and Richard discussing it one night in the kitchen after dinner. He'd said to Mom, "I've only raised daughters. What kinds of things do I *do* with a boy?"

"Oh, Richard, don't be such a worry wart," Mom answered. "Jeff will think of something. He has a very active imagination. Just let him lead you."

Mom's right about Jeff. He is the kind of kid

who likes to do a hundred things — all at once. When I visited Dad and Jeff in California, the three of us went to Disneyland and Jeff raced from ride to ride, making sure we rode every single one.

"Jeff also loves sports," Mom had said. "Maybe you two can toss a baseball around."

"Hmmm," Richard mumbled. "Maybe."

Mom seemed to have forgotten that Richard is totally unathletic. He doesn't play any sports, and he doesn't watch football or baseball games on TV. He's just not interested in them.

Anyway, I was glad that Jeff and Richard were going to have the chance to get to know each other better. It's important to me that my brother like Richard and that Richard like Jeff.

"Oh, girls," Richard said as he left the room, "you've put a lot of work into making the house look nice. Let's try to keep it that way until Jeff gets here."

"That's fine with me, Dad," Mary Anne said as she put the cap back on the spray furniture polish. "I like a clean house."

I know Mary Anne didn't mean for her comment to sound like a dig at my mom, but it did. Just a little bit. Of course, I didn't really mind. Putting two completely different families together in the same house has been hard.

But we're learning to live with each others' quirks. And even to joke about them.

"We should take a picture of this room and the rest of the house," I giggled. "So when things get messy again, we'll remember what they were supposed to look like."

Mary Anne opened her mouth to respond, but what we heard instead was "Meow!"

"What?" I asked.

"I didn't say anything," Mary Anne replied. "It was Tigger."

Tigger is Mary Anne's gray striped kitten. He can usually be found sleeping on Mary Anne's bed, but today was different. He had followed Mary Anne from room to room, meowing, as if to say, "What's all the commotion about?"

"Meow!"

I spun in a circle looking for Tigger. "Where is he?"

Mary Anne peered under the bed. "I'm not sure. I can hear him, but I can't see him. Here Tiggy. Come on, Mousekin." (Mary Anne has about a zillion names for Tigger.)

"Meow! Meow!"

"I think it's coming from over there." I pointed to the closet. "You don't think . . ."

Before I could finish my sentence Mary Anne had opened the closet door and scooped Tigger up in her arms. "Not again!" she murmured. "You silly kitty. I thought you'd never go in a closet again, after what happened with Kerry Bruno."

Kerry is Logan Bruno's little sister. Who's Logan? Mary Anne's boyfriend. He's really good looking and has this soft southern accent because he's from Kentucky. He and Mary Anne have been going steady for a long time. They did split up when Mary Anne thought Logan was taking over her life, but they got back together again and they're fine now. Anyway, when the Brunos first moved to Stoneybrook, Logan's sister was lonely and wanted a pet. Kerry found Tigger outside and took him to her house and hid him in her closet for five whole days. It was very scary and Mary Anne was really upset.

"Maybe Tigger was planning to surprise Jeff," I joked. "You know, jump out of the closet when he arrived and yell, 'Meow!' "

Mary Anne giggled and shook her head. "No. He'd yell, 'Purrsprise!' "

That did it. Mary Anne and I laughed so hard that we collapsed onto Jeff's perfectly made bed. It got wrinkled, but it didn't matter. My brother would be here soon and I was happy.

CHAPTER 2

"The wheels on the bus go round and round,
round and round, round and round.
The wheels on the bus go round and round,
all around the town."

Five-year-old Suzi Barrett and her sister Marnie were sitting in a cardboard box on the Barretts' front porch when I arrived to baby-sit on Saturday afternoon.

"Hi, Dawn!" Suzi called. "Look at me. I'm the bus driver."

At that moment, the front door flew open and out raced Suzi's eight-year-old brother, Buddy. He grabbed the cardboard box and started dragging it across the porch. "Hey, Dawn. Guess what I am."

I shrugged. "I give up."

"I'm the tow truck," he said. "This bus broke down."

"It did not." Suzi batted at his hands, trying to make him let go of the box.

"Did too."

"Did not."

Marnie, who had been quietly listening to Buddy and Suzi argue, suddenly stood up in the box and ordered, "Stop! I want out."

I shook my head and giggled. Baby-sitting for the Barretts can be like stepping into the middle of a tornado. I used to call them the Impossible Three because they were so out of control. Then I discovered the problem wasn't the kids, it was Mrs. Barrett, who had gone through a really tough divorce. She was so busy trying to find a job and straighten out her own life that she didn't have enough time for the children. But that's changed. She's happy now and the kids, who really are nice, have settled down. Sort of.

"Dawn!" Suzi cried, starting to pout. "Tell Buddy to let go of my bus."

Even though Mrs. Barrett hadn't left yet, I realized it was time to take charge. I hopped onto the porch. "Buddy, there's a red light. What do tow truck drivers do when they see one?"

Buddy let go of the box and yelled, "Stop!"

"Good." I smiled at him and ruffled his hair. Then I whispered to Marnie, "Say, ding ding."

"Ding! Ding!" Marnie shouted.

11

"What's that mean?" Suzi asked.

"It means one of your passengers wants to get off the bus," I said. "You had better open the doors and let her out."

Suzi, who loves to pretend, made a swooshing sound and opened the door. "Okay, passenger," she said. "You dinged, so get off."

Marnie didn't budge. Now the game was getting fun for her. She beamed at me and sang, "Ding, ding! Ding, ding!"

Buddy tugged on the sleeve of my jacket. "She won't get off the bus. Want me to arrest her?"

"I thought you were the tow truck driver," I said.

"No." Buddy shook his head. "Now I'm the sheriff."

"And I'm his deputy," Suzi added.

Luckily, Mrs. Barrett appeared at the front door before things became too confusing. She looked like a model. I'm not kidding. She was wearing cream-colored linen slacks, a blazer, and a lavender silk blouse with a pearl necklace and earrings.

"You look wonderful," I told her.

"Oh, do you think so?" she asked, nervously patting her wavy hair. "Franklin DeWitt is taking me to Chez Maurice for dinner."

"Chez Maurice is one of my favorite restaurants," I said. "We always go there for really special occasions, like Mom's birthday or when Mom and Richard got married."

"It's Franklin's favorite, too. He knows Maurice," Mrs. Barrett said. Her cheeks flushed a little brighter pink as she spoke.

"The number of the restaurant is on the bulletin board in the kitchen," Mrs. Barrett explained as she checked the tiny gold watch circling her wrist. "There're French fries and hamburger patties in the freezer for the kids' dinner. You can have them eat in about half an hour."

"All right." I was really impressed at how organized Mrs. Barrett had become. When I first baby-sat for her, she was a disaster. Sometimes she forgot to tell me where she was going or when she'd be home. Her house was always messy, so I ended up doing her housework. I even planned the meals. It was really too much for me. So, after serious discussions with the BSC, I finally had a talk with Mrs. Barrett. Now it's amazing how much she's changed.

"I'm meeting Franklin downtown. We're just going to dinner and then coming right home." She smiled at her three children. "Franklin wants to spend time with the kids."

"Great!" Buddy cried. "We can kick the soccer ball around. Or maybe wrestle. We did that last week and it was fun!"

Mrs. Barrett looked extra pleased that Buddy felt that way about Franklin, which made me realize her new relationship was pretty serious.

We waved good-bye to Mrs. Barrett, and before the kids could return to their game of the sheriff versus the bus passenger, I said, "What do you say we go inside and play?"

"But I want to wait for Franklin," Suzi said.

"They're going to a restaurant first. Then they're coming home," I explained. "Hey, I've got an idea. Why don't we eat dinner while they're eating. We can pretend we're in a restaurant, just like Franklin and your mom."

The kids liked that idea. We spent the next three hours playing restaurant. First we made menus using crayons and notebook paper. Buddy and Suzi drew pictures of their favorite foods.

"What kind of food is that?" I asked Suzi as she carefully drew big red circles all over her paper.

"Hamburger," she replied. "And pizza and donuts."

It was hard for me not to wince. Like I said, I don't eat red meat or fatty foods.

"How about you, Buddy?" I asked. "What are you drawing on your menu?"

Buddy drew a stick man holding a hot dog. "This is Franklin," he said. "Eating a hot dog. I like hot dogs. Franklin gave us hot dogs last week."

"Oh, did you go to his house?" I asked as I drew my own pictures of a spinach salad with avocado slices on whole wheat toast.

"No." Buddy shook his head. "I don't know where he lives."

"Did your mom meet him at work?"

Buddy shrugged. "I don't think so. I don't know where he works. But he sure is funny."

"Franklin gives me horseback rides," Suzi said cheerfully. Then she picked up a blue crayon. "I'm going to put a horse on my menu."

"Horsies!" Marnie cried.

Franklin sounded like a fun person. And just what the Barrett children needed. "I wonder if he has any kids," I murmured out loud.

"I haven't seen any," Buddy said as he put the finishing touches on his menu. Then he held it up. "Ta da!" He had folded the paper in half and on the front he'd drawn a picture of a boy with a bubble coming out of his mouth. In the bubble he'd written, *My Food by Buddy Barrett. Yumm.*

After making the menus, the kids were ready to eat dinner. I served their food, pretending to be a waiter. I think they enjoyed ordering me around.

"Oh, miss!" Buddy called from the kitchen table. "I need catsup on my hamburger. And mustard. And pickle relish."

"Me too, missus," Suzi added.

Marnie just banged on her plastic plate with her fork chanting, "Fries! Fries!"

After dinner was over, we washed the dishes and were just sitting down to watch a Disney singalong video when the front door opened.

Mrs. Barrett, still looking as pretty and perfect as before, stepped into the front hall. Behind her was a very tall man with auburn hair and wire-rimmed glasses. He flashed a warm smile at the children.

"Hi, kids," he said in a deep friendly voice. "How are you doing?" Then he crossed to me and shook my hand. "You must be Dawn. I'm Franklin DeWitt."

I shook his hand. "Pleased to meet you, Mr. DeWitt."

"Natalie said you saved her life not long ago."

I could feel my cheeks heat up. "I just helped Mrs. Barrett get a little better organized, that's all."

Franklin grinned. "Well, I'm glad to meet you."

Then he turned his attention back to the kids. He pulled a paper bag out of his jacket pocket. "Can anyone guess what I've got in this bag? Could it be an elephant?"

"Noooooo!" all three kids shouted.

"A hippopotamus?"

"Nooooooo."

"How about a kazoo?"

"A kazoo?" Buddy asked. "Is that some kind of animal?"

"No." Franklin Dewitt chuckled. "It's a musical instrument. I brought three of them. We're going to make a band."

While the kids giggled and tooted on their kazoos, Mrs. Barrett paid me. She hummed while she wrote the check. I was glad to see the Barrett bunch so happy.

In fact, I was so glad that I went straight home and made one of my favorite dishes: pasta with fresh veggies. I remembered that it was also one of Jeff's favorites. Thinking about my brother suddenly made me want to talk to him. So I picked up the phone and dialed.

Two rings.

"Schafers. This is Jeff."

Just hearing my brother's voice, I got a warm feeling inside me, like hot chocolate on a cold night. "Hi, Jeff, it's me."

"Dawn!" He sounded happy to hear from

me. "I'm doing the countdown. Five days until I get on that Boeing 767. I can't wait."

"Do you think you'll get to watch a movie?" I asked, settling back in my chair with my food.

"I hope so, but it'll probably be something really dorky like *The Care Bears Meet the Smurfs*."

It's a good thing no one was around because I snorted with laughter and my pasta shot everywhere.

"Dawn, are you still there?" Jeff asked, knocking the receiver against the table.

"I'm here, goofball," I said. "You just made me toss my dinner."

"Hey, sounds like you need a barf bag. I'll pick one up for you on my trip over."

The last time Jeff flew, he collected every salt and pepper packet and dairy creamer container that he could find on the plane and put them all in an air sickness bag, which he proudly displayed on his dresser.

"Jeff!" a voice called from the background. "Dinner's ready."

"Who's that?" I asked. "Mrs. Bruen?"

"Yeah," Jeff said. "She made vegetable lasagna for me." (Mrs. Bruen is Dad's housekeeper.)

For a moment I had forgotten about the three-hour time difference. It was eight o'clock

18

in Connecticut but five on the West Coast.

"I'll let you go eat. I just wanted to tell you I plan on having an absolute blast with you."

"We better!" There was a pause and then Jeff said, softly, "I really miss you, Dawn."

I felt this lump in my throat and my eyes got all misty. "Me too. Give Dad a big hug and kiss for me."

"See you Friday!"

I couldn't wait.

CHAPTER 3

"Come on, Dawn!" Mary Anne shouted up the stairs. "The BSC meeting starts in ten minutes. We're going to be late."

"Not if we run." I leapt down the stairs and the two of us raced out our front door. We had exactly nine minutes to reach Claudia Kishi's house or suffer the wrath of Kristy!

Claud's digital clock was turning from 5:29 to 5:30 when we raced into the room. Mary Anne fell on the bed and I collapsed on the carpet by Claud's desk as Kristy announced, "This meeting of the Baby-sitters Club has officially started."

Okay. Now is a good time to tell you about the BSC. It's really more of a business than a club. We meet three times a week at Claudia Kishi's house from 5:30 till 6:00. People call during our meetings if they need a sitter. And because so many of us are here they're practically guaranteed one. Isn't that a great idea?

Call one number and reach seven experienced, responsible baby-sitters.

The BSC was Kristy Thomas's great idea. That's one of the reasons she's president. Kristy is a real leader type and she's very organized. Besides heading the BSC, she also coaches a little kids' softball team called Kristy's Krushers. Some people would call Kristy a tomboy. She certainly dresses like one: jeans, a sweater over a turtleneck, sneakers, and sometimes a baseball cap. (It's practically her uniform.) Here's something you'd never guess about Kristy — she's rich. Her mom married Watson Brewer, this millionaire, and now they all live in his mansion. It's huge! I guess that's good, because on some weekends ten people live there. There're Watson and his two children Andrew and Karen, Kristy, her mom, and her three brothers, David Michael, Charlie, and Sam. And Emily Michelle, the Vietnamese baby Mr. and Mrs. Brewer adopted (she's adorable). Plus Nannie, Kristy's grandmother, who moved in to help take care of all of those kids. That's a lot of people!

Our club vice-president is Claudia Kishi. We hold the meetings at her house because she has a phone in her room with her very own private number. Isn't that cool? Claud is about as different from Kristy as you can get. Claudia could care less about sports. What she loves is art. And it shows in everything she does or wears. Today for instance she was dressed in black overalls that she had splattered with pink and green and yellow globs of paint. Her purple high top tennis shoes matched her purple long sleeve T-shirt. Claud has beautiful black shining hair that she'd fixed in a French braid. On top of her head perched a little white painter's cap that she'd also splattered with paint. She looked awesome. (She always does.) Claud is Japanese-American and has these beautiful almond-shaped eyes and a perfect ivory complexion. I don't know how she manages it because she is an absolute junk food fiend. I'm not kidding. She hides chips and candy all over her room. One thing about Claud you should know. She's very smart, but for some reason she does terribly in school. She just can't spell. And to make things worse, her sister, Janine, is a genius and always gets straight A's. (Claud struggles along with C's.) One other thing about Claud — Stacey McGill is her best friend.

Stacey is our club treasurer because she's a real math whiz. Once a week she collects dues from us which we use to help pay Claudia's phone bill and to buy supplies for our Kid-Kits (more about those later). Stacey has huge blue eyes with thick dark lashes and fluffy blonde hair that her mother lets her perm.

Stacey is a super trendy dresser. She used to live in New York City (her dad still does), which I think helped make her so sophisticated. Stacey's parents are divorced, like mine, and she lives with her mom in the house just behind Mallory Pike, one of our junior officers. Stacey is really thin, mostly because she has to stay on a strict diet. You see, Stacey is diabetic. Her body can't process sugar, which means NO SWEETS. She has to give herself these shots (ew, ick!) of insulin every day. If she doesn't, she could get really sick. The neat thing about Stacey is she doesn't let her illness get her down. She's really funny and nice and I like her a lot.

Mary Anne is our club secretary which, in my opinion, is the toughest job. She keeps the record book that contains phone numbers and addresses of our clients, an appointment calendar, and a list of our earnings. Mary Anne has to keep track of all of our schedules so, when a client calls, she can assign the jobs. And here's the truly amazing thing about Mary Anne. She has never made a mistake. I already told you that Mary Anne is sweet and sensitive. She's also a great listener. Even though she's shy and kind of quiet, Mary Anne was the first member of the BSC to have a steady boyfriend.

There are two junior officers in the BSC,

Mallory Pike and Jessica Ramsey. They're junior because they're in the sixth grade (the rest of us are in the eighth grade). Mal and Jessi are best friends, probably because they have a lot in common. They both are the oldest kid in their family, they love to read, and are crazy about anything that has to do with horses. They love horse movies (*The Black Stallion*, *Wild Hearts Can't Be Broken*), horse books (especially anything by Marguerite Henry), and even old horse TV shows (*Mr. Ed*). Mal and Jessi are also very different. For instance, Jessi is black and Mal is white. Mal has seven — *seven* — younger brothers and sisters (three of them are triplets). Jessi has only two — Becca and her baby brother Squirt. Jessi plans to be a professional ballerina with a famous dance company like the American Ballet Theatre. I'm sure she'll do it. She's already danced the lead in several ballets at her dance school. Mal loves to write and plans to be an author and illustrator of children's books. Isn't that cool?

I'm the alternate officer which means that I fill in for anyone who's sick or on vacation. Let's see. I think I've covered everyone in the BSC except our associate members, Logan Bruno (Mary Anne's boyfriend) and Shannon Kilbourne. Shannon is a friend of Kristy's and has been coming to a lot of our meetings lately.

Who knows? Maybe someday she'll become a permanent member.

Back to the meeting. While we waited at Claud's for the phone to ring, Stacey made an announcement. "Okay, everybody guess what day this is. Dues day."

She was answered by loud groans from us.

"I know it hurts to part with your money, but fork it over. We need to buy some new Crayola packs and coloring books for the Kid-Kits. Everyone is running low."

What are Kid-Kits? They're another one of Kristy's great ideas (of course!). We each painted a cardboard carton and decorated it with glitter and sequins and beads and anything else Claudia could find. Then we filled it with old toys, puzzles, and crayons. We usually take them with us when we go on jobs and the kids love them. (It's much more fun to play with someone else's toys than their own.)

"Ahem." Kristy folded her arms across her chest and gave us each her stern look. "I would just like to say that the club notebook hasn't been touched in over a week. You guys better start writing or you'll never catch up."

The club notebook is really more like a diary in which we're each supposed to write up every job we go on. Then we pass the notebook around so we can find out what's happening with our clients. Mal and Kristy really like writing in the notebook. But the rest of us think it's kind of a pain. Not all of the jobs are that interesting. Of course, it can be very helpful. We discover things like the fact that Marnie Barrett is allergic to chocolate or that the Arnold twins hate dressing alike and being called cute.

Brrrring!

Stacey was closest to the phone so she answered.

"Baby-sitters Club. What can we do for you? Oh, hi, Mrs. Barrett."

Stacey listened for a few minutes nodding and saying "Mm hmm." Finally she said, "We'll check the appointment book and call you right back."

Stacey hung up the phone and frowned. "That's strange."

"Ooh, what?" I love a mystery.

"Well, that was Mrs. Barrett on the phone but she didn't sound like herself. She sounded sort of giggly and shy."

"What does she need?" Mary Anne asked, flipping open the notebook.

"A sitter for Saturday because she and someone named Franklin will be going on a family picnic together."

"Franklin is her new boyfriend," I explained

26

to my friends. "I met him on Saturday and he's really nice and a lot of fun."

"He also has four kids," Stacey said.

"Four kids!" I practically shouted. "I didn't know that."

"About the age of the Barrett kids. Mrs. Barrett said she and Franklin want their children to meet each other."

"Wait a minute." Kristy ticked off the numbers on her fingers. "That's nine people."

"Right." Stacey nodded. "That's why Mrs. Barrett needs a sitter."

Mary Anne, who had been checking the notebook, said, "Claud has an art class, Jessi has a ballet lesson, Stacey is sitting for the Perkinses, and Dawn and I can't do it because Jeff's coming to visit." She raised her head. "That leaves Kristy and Mallory."

Kristy straightened her visor. "Sorry. Bart and I planned to go over some new techniques for teaching kids how to bat."

Mallory grinned. "Looks like it's me. That would be fine. I'm used to big groups of kids."

Claudia, who was busy tearing open a package of Ring-Dings that she'd found in the bottom drawer of her dresser, suddenly gasped. "I wonder if there's a special reason for this get-together."

Mary Anne (who I told you is a mushy person) clasped her hands together and sighed.

"Maybe they're going to get married. Wouldn't that be romantic?" she said.

"Boy, if they did that," Stacey said, "it'd be like that old show *The Brady Bunch*."

"It would be like having an instant baseball team," Kristy added. (Leave it to her to think of sports.)

"It would be crazy," Claudia said, shaking her head. "Just think about it. All of those kids trying to get into the bathroom, fighting over which TV show to watch, and drinking gallons of milk and soda."

"It's not so bad if you're organized," Mal said. "Dinners can be a lot of fun — almost like a party. And with so many people around, you never feel lonely."

"Mrs. Barrett really seems happy," I told my friends. "And the kids really like Franklin."

All of this was interesting. Very interesting indeed.

CHAPTER 4

Have you ever noticed that when you want time to go fast, it suddenly slows down? That's what was happening during the BSC meeting on Friday afternoon. It seemed like every parent in Stoneybrook called. Stacey made an announcement about the supplies for the Kid-Kits. Jessi told us about the open house her ballet school was having. And still the meeting didn't end.

"Mary Anne," I whispered. "What time is it?"

"One minute later than the last time you asked me," Mary Anne whispered back. "It's ten minutes to six."

Kristy, who was trying to discuss new methods of advertising, shot us one of her "quiet down" looks.

I was too excited to be quiet. I could barely sit still. It was Friday. Jeff's arrival day. The plan was for Mary Anne and me to rush home

29

after the BSC meeting, eat dinner, and then drive to the airport with our parents.

"So what do you think, Dawn?" Kristy asked me. I realized she'd gone around the room asking for everyone's opinion of her advertising plan. Now she'd reached me and I hadn't been paying attention.

I cleared my throat and tried to pretend I'd heard her plan. "I think it's an excellent idea. Of course you always have great ideas, Kristy."

Claudia, Stacey, Mal, and Jessi started giggling. Kristy just looked confused.

"What's so funny?" I asked.

"Kristy wanted to know if the new BSC fliers should be pink or green," Claud answered. "And you said that's an excellent idea."

"I'm sorry, everybody," I said. "But my brother is coming today. I'm having a little trouble concentrating."

"Obviously," Kristy replied sternly. Then her expression softened. "I bet you're really excited."

"Definitely."

"What are you planning to do while he's here?" Jessi asked.

"We'll go out to dinner, play video games, watch some scary movies, and talk," I said, feeling little bubbles of happiness fizz inside of me.

"At the end of the week, we're all going on a four-day vacation. Either to Washington D.C. or Boston," Mary Anne added.

Brrring!

"Baby-sitters Club," Stacey said, picking up the phone. "Oh, hi, Mrs. Spier."

It was my mom. I shot Mary Anne a worried look. Maybe something had gone wrong. Maybe Jeff couldn't come.

"No, they're still here," Stacey said, smiling at us. "All right. I'll tell them. 'Bye."

Stacey hung up the phone and grinned. "Your mom's really excited. She wanted me to tell you to be sure and come straight home and remind you that Jeff's plane will arrive in less than two hours."

Mary Anne shook her head. "She already told us that last night at dinner and before we left for school this morning. Jeff had better get here before Dawn and her mom turn into complete Looney Toons."

I was about to protest when I caught sight of Claud's digital clock. It said 6:01. The meeting should have been over a whole minute ago. "Oh, no! We're late," I cried, springing to my feet. "Come on, Mary Anne. We have to get home."

I dragged Mary Anne to the door. As we were leaving she called over her shoulder to the rest of the BSC, "See, what did I tell you guys? Dawn has completely lost her mind."

Mom had avocado and cheese melts waiting for us when we got home. I don't even remember eating mine. Mary Anne and I quickly cleared the table and before we knew it, my family was all in the car heading for the airport.

On the way, Mom and I amused ourselves by wondering what Jeff would look like and what he'd be wearing.

"I say he'll have sun-bleached hair that'll look sort of spiky. And he'll be wearing his favorite green-and-white striped T-shirt and jeans."

Mom shook her head. "I'm sure he's outgrown that shirt. Remember, Dawn, it's been a few months since we've seen him. Boys Jeff's age sprout overnight."

We were silent for a little bit, thinking about how sad it was that Jeff was growing up and we weren't out us there to watch him.

Richard cleared his throat and adjusted his glasses as he drove. "I've been trying to plan activities for Jeff while you girls are in school, but I'm having a little difficulty. Maybe you can think of something."

"Take him to the mall," Mary Anne suggested. "He might like that."

"Or to a movie," I said. "Jeff loves movies. Especially scary ones."

Mom patted Richard on the knee. "Now don't be nervous. You and Jeff will have a wonderful time. I'm sure of it."

Time suddenly started speeding up because all of a sudden, we reached the airport. Richard dropped us in front of the terminal and I raced to look at the check-in counter. Jeff's flight number was flashing. That meant his plane was just landing.

"He's here," I squealed. "Mary Anne! Mom! Jeff's here!"

Mom's eyes filled with tears. "Come on, girls. Let's go get your brother."

The passengers were just starting to step off the plane when we reached the gate. First an old couple came through the gate, then a woman with three squirming children, then a teenager carrying a guitar. Finally a boy in a green-and-white striped T-shirt, jeans, and spiky sun-bleached hair appeared in the doorway.

"Mom!" I yelled. "Jeff didn't have a growth spurt. He looks just the same, and he's wearing his favorite shirt."

Suddenly Jeff pushed through the crowd

and was in our arms. "Mom, Dawn!" he cried, wrapping his arms around us and giving us big bear hugs. "I'm here. I'm really here."

Mary Anne and Richard, who'd joined us, hung back for only a second and then they hugged Jeff, too. "The flight was great," Jeff said. "They gave me the cheese plate. It had these neat little toothpicks — " He reached into the fanny pack he was wearing and held up two green plastic toothpicks with a tiny airplane on top. "I also got the kid fun pack. See? It has a deck of cards, a pack of crayons, and this cool Robin Hood comic book. Hey, are you ready for this? The flight attendant also handed out special barf bags for kids. I'm not kidding. Look. Mine's got cartoons all over it."

I draped my arm around Jeff's shoulder and giggled. "You haven't changed one bit."

Jeff was so excited about being back in Stoneybrook that he chattered nonstop all the way to our house.

"Can you believe it?" he asked as he settled into the seat between Mary Anne and me. "No homework for a whole week."

Mom turned around in her seat. "I bought your favorite frozen yogurt."

"Double chocolate chip?" Jeff's eyes widened. "All right, Mom!"

He gave her a high-five and I actually saw

Mom blush. She was so thrilled that Jeff was home.

"I hope you got plenty of supplies because the Pike triplets will probably be spending a lot of time at our house," Jeff added.

"Did you write to them?" I asked.

"No," he said. "But that doesn't matter. I wonder if they like soccer? Everyone at my school is playing it."

"I don't think I've ever heard them discuss it," Mary Anne said. "I think baseball is their sport."

"That's right," I added. "They're in Little League."

That didn't seem to faze Jeff. He plunged ahead. "I think I'll call those guys as soon as we get home. I want to go hiking, and ride bikes, and explore the secret passage."

"Again?" I asked.

"Sure," Jeff replied. "Maybe this time we really will see a ghost."

"I hope not," Mary Anne said with a shudder.

" 'Fraidy cat," Jeff teased goodnaturedly. He tickled her in the side. "Wimp."

"Stop," Mary Anne said, giggling. "I am not a wimp. I just don't like ghosts."

Richard, who was enjoying our chatter, called over his shoulder, "Jeff, we're all going on a trip next weekend. But we can't decide whether to go to Boston or Washington D.C. Where do you think we should go?"

"I don't know," Jeff said. "Washington's got all those cool monuments and the Aerospace Museum. But Boston has that neat old ship."

"*Old Ironsides*," Richard said over his shoulder. "The oldest commissioned warship in the world."

"It also has the Franklin Park Zoo, trolley rides, and whale watching," Mom added.

"Whales? I love whales!" Jeff cried.

"But Washington D.C. has the Smithsonian Institution," Mary Anne pointed out. "Which is one of the all-time great museums."

"That's true," Richard said. "If we went to Washington, we could probably watch the Senate in action and maybe even tour the White House."

"Do you think we'd see the President?" Jeff asked.

Richard chuckled. "I doubt it. But we would probably see a lot of people who work for him."

"Like Secret Service guys," I added, knowing Jeff would really like that.

"Well, we have a few days to decide," my mother said. "In the meantime, Richard and I have a big surprise for you."

"What is it?" the three of us asked.

"Next Sunday, I've arranged for a photographer to come to our house and take a family portrait."

"A portrait?" Jeff repeated. "You mean a photo?"

"Same thing." My mom laughed. "Only this one will be very large. I plan to have it framed and put over our mantelpiece."

"Ooh, that's beautiful," Mary Anne said. I knew without even looking at Mary Anne that tears were probably welling in her eyes. She can get so sappy over things like this. However, I was feeling a little misty-eyed myself. Jeff was back with our family. We were going to have two days off from school, and we had a fantastic trip to look forward to. Things couldn't have been better.

CHAPTER 5

Saturday

I was really looking forward to baby-sitting for the Barrett kids. Mrs. Barrett and Franklin had planned to take all seven of their kids to the petting zoo and then to a children's play, with a picnic in between. Sounds fun, huh? It wasn't. From the moment I arrived at the Barrett house, things didn't feel right. First of all Buddy was unusually quiet, and he is NEVER quiet. And because Buddy was acting weird, Marnie and Suzi were acting the same. Plus Mrs. Barrett, who usually seems so cool and collected, was a nervous wreck. Things went downhill from there...

Buddy Barrett was sitting cross-legged on the top step of the front porch when Mallory arrived to baby-sit. He stared down at the ground, his chin in his hands. Suzi sat slumped next to him, clutching a doll.

"Hey, Buddy. Hey, Suzi," Mallory said as she trotted up their front walk. "What's the matter?"

Buddy shrugged. "We're waiting for *them*."

"Them? You mean Mr. DeWitt's children?"

Buddy nodded. "I don't know why they have to come over here. I liked Franklin better by himself."

Suzi looked at her brother, then folded her arms across her chest and stuck out her lower lip. "Me, too."

"You guys are going to have fun," Mallory said. "Aren't his kids about your age?"

Buddy shrugged again. "I don't know."

Mallory had never seen the Barrett kids so glum. She decided she had to do something to put them in a good mood *fast* — or the afternoon would be a disaster.

"Come on, let's go inside. I want to show you something."

Buddy and Suzi followed Mal into the house and the three of them nearly collided with Mrs. Barrett. Her arms were loaded with a picnic basket, two blankets, an umbrella, and a Thermos. "Oh, Mallory, am I glad you're here. Help!"

Mallory rushed forward and caught the Thermos just before it hit the floor. "Are you okay, Mrs. Barrett?"

"I'm supposed to make lunch for ten people. How do I do that? I can barely make dinner for four."

Mrs. Barrett's hair, which usually looks perfect, had fallen over one eye. And she hadn't put on her lipstick yet. "Franklin will be here in ten minutes." She groaned. "I just don't know what to do."

"Look, why don't you finish getting ready and I'll pack the lunch," Mallory suggested. "What are you planning to make?"

"Sandwiches, but I don't know what Franklin's children like to eat. What if I guess wrong?"

"Do what my mom does," Mallory said. "Pack a loaf of bread, peanut butter, jelly, and slices of cheese and ham. Then everyone can make their own."

"That's so simple." Mrs. Barrett shook her head. "Now why didn't I think of that?"

"It sounds like you have a lot on your mind," Mallory said, hoping to make Mrs. Barrett feel more comfortable. "If you've got some apples, I'll pack those. We'll just cut slices for dessert."

Mrs. Barrett gave Mallory a hug. "You're a lifesaver," she exclaimed, running up the stairs.

Mallory felt a tug at the sleeve of her windbreaker. Buddy and Suzi were staring up at her expectantly.

"What were you going to show us?" Suzi asked.

Mallory hit her forehead with the heel of her hand. "I almost forgot. I wanted to show you two how to make hats to wear on the picnic."

"Hats?" Buddy made a face. "But I already have one."

"I bet you don't have a pirate hat," Mallory said, mysteriously. "That you have to make special. Do you have any old newspapers?"

Suzi and Buddy raced off to find some. Meanwhile Marnie, who had been sitting in the high chair in the kitchen eating a cracker, began to cry.

"More," she wailed.

Mallory got Marnie another cracker from an open box in the cupboard and stuck it in her hand. Then she raced around the kitchen, pulling open cupboards and tossing different food items into Mrs. Barrett's picnic basket.

"We found some paper," Buddy declared as he and Suzi burst into the kitchen, their arms full of old newspapers.

"All right," Mal said, closing the basket lid. "Sit at the table and I'll show you how to fold a pirate's hat."

Ten minutes later, Buddy and Suzi were sporting triangle-shaped hats as they munched on the saltines Mallory had gotten out for Marnie. They were still quieter than usual but they seemed content. For the moment.

Ding-dong.

Buddy and Suzi turned to each other and whispered loudly, "They're here!"

BARROOO!

Pow, the Barretts' basset hound, who had been sound asleep on the living room couch, sprang into action. He galloped into the foyer, nearly tripping Mrs. Barrett as she hurried to open the front door. Standing on the front porch was Franklin DeWitt and his four children: eight-year-old Lindsey, six-year-old Taylor, four-year-old Madeleine, and two-year-old Ryan.

Mrs. Barrett smiled warmly. "Franklin, come in — "

"Aaaahhhh!" Ryan took one look at Pow and leapt into Franklin's arms.

Mallory quickly dragged Pow by the collar

into the kitchen. When she returned to the foyer, she found Mrs. Barrett and Franklin introducing their kids to each other. It was pretty clear that Franklin's children weren't very excited about meeting the Barrett kids. The seven of them stood silently, staring at each other, which made Mrs. Barrett even more nervous.

"Well," she said, in an overly cheery voice, "you kids will have plenty of time to talk in the car. We better get going."

But when the two families opened the doors to Franklin's car, they realized they wouldn't fit.

"Oh, dear," Franklin said, scratching his head. "I forgot there are ten of us. Seven kids, two parents, and a baby-sitter. We need a bus to handle this big a crew."

"We'll just take two cars," Mrs. Barrett suggested. Then she clapped her hands together and asked, "Who wants to ride in which car?"

The DeWitt children huddled around their father while Buddy whispered to Mallory, "I don't want to ride with them."

Mrs. Barrett shrugged at Franklin. "I'll take my kids and Mallory. You take yours and we'll just follow you to Lawrenceville."

"Sounds good to me," Franklin said. "All right, kids. All aboard!"

As they followed Franklin out of Stoneybrook and onto the highway heading north,

Mallory tried to make conversation with the kids. "Lindsey looked really nice," she said to Buddy. "And I bet she's in your grade."

"Who cares?" he mumbled.

Mrs. Barrett made a sour face in the mirror. "Buddy, don't talk like that. Mallory's right. Lindsey does seem like a nice girl, and Taylor looks fun, too. If you just give them a chance, I'm sure you kids will — "

The rest of her sentence was cut off by a loud explosion from the passenger side of the car.

"What was that?" Suzi yelled.

She was answered by the *ker-thump*, *ker-thump* of a flat front tire.

"I-I can't believe it," Mrs. Barrett spluttered. "I just can't believe it."

"Honk your horn, Mrs. Barrett," Mallory said. "So Mr. DeWitt will know you have to stop."

Mrs. Barrett beeped the horn, then pulled off to the side of the road. Luckily Franklin saw her and was able to pull over and walk back to her car.

While Franklin and Mrs. Barrett changed the tire, Mallory watched the kids. She spread a blanket on the grass by the side of the road for them to sit on. What amazed her was how quiet they were.

"Do you guys want to sing a song?" Mal

asked, trying to think of something entertaining.

No response.

"We could play a game." Mallory racked her brain to remember the car games her family played on long trips. "We could play Alphabet Plates. We look for license plates from states like Alabama and Arkansas and then work our way through the alphabet. And the first person to get the closest to Wyoming wins."

"Okay," Buddy said. "I'll try it."

Franklin's children exchanged quiet looks, then nodded in agreement. Mallory remembered that the younger kids couldn't read yet so she added a twist to the game. "And for you guys, first we'll look for a red car, and then a blue, and a green, and so on."

The kids smiled wanly. Mallory was relieved when Franklin finally got the spare tire on Mrs. Barrett's car and they could load up again.

However, when they arrived at the petting zoo, all of the picnic tables were occupied.

"This is incredible," Franklin said, squinting at the rows of tables filled with families. "It's never this crowded. Ever."

"Mommy, I'm hungry," Suzi said, hungrily eyeing the plate of fried chicken on a nearby picnic table.

"Me, too, Daddy," Madeleine cried. "I want

to eat." She tugged on her father's pant leg. "Now!"

"We'd *all* like to eat," Franklin said. "But there aren't any picnic tables. And the ground is gravel, so we can't very well sit on it."

Mallory shifted the picnic basket she was carrying. "I've got a suggestion," she volunteered. "Why don't we make the sandwiches out here in the parking lot? Then the kids can carry them when we walk through the zoo."

"Excellent idea!" Franklin said. He turned in a circle and spotted a little patch of grass by the front entrance. "We'll make lunch right over there."

Mallory, Mrs. Barrett, and Franklin set up a sandwich assembly line that was lots of fun for the kids. They started a contest to see who could make the thickest peanut butter-and-jelly sandwich. Finally everyone was holding a sandwich in one hand and a paper cup of apple juice in the other.

"Are we ready to visit the wild kingdom?" Franklin joked.

"Yes!" the children cheered. "Let's go."

For a second, Mallory thought they might have a pleasant afternoon after all. But that ended the moment they reached the petting zoo. A goat snatched Madeleine's sandwich out of her hand and swallowed it in one gulp.

"Daddy!" she howled. "That rotten goat stole my food."

That set Ryan off. "Pick me up, Daddy!"

"Here's my sandwich," Franklin said to Madeleine. "Eat that." Then he scooped Ryan up in his arms. "There's nothing to be afraid of, son. Goats are harmless."

"I'm scared," Ryan cried, burying his nose in his father's shoulder.

The strain was starting to show in Franklin's voice as he patted his son's back. "Okay, calm down," he said hoarsely. "They're just ordinary goats and chickens. You don't need to cry."

"Daddy," Taylor said, tugging on his father's sleeve. "Let's go into the barn. The Clydesdale horses are there."

Mrs. Barrett nodded at Franklin. "Good idea."

It took a few minutes to herd two strollers and seven children out of the corral area and into the barn. Once they were inside, the kids started complaining again.

"It stinks in here," Lindsey said, pinching her nose.

"And it's dark," Taylor added.

"I'm hot," Suzi said.

"There are too many people," Buddy grumbled. "I can't see."

The air in the barn was heavy and the crowd

of people huddling around the horse stalls made even Mallory start to feel a little claustrophobic. Finally, the people crowding in front moved and the others could step forward. That's when Marnie threw up.

"Oh, gross," Suzi cried, springing away from her sister. "Marnie got sick."

Mrs. Barrett was starting to look more than a little frazzled. "Franklin, I think we should cut this visit short and go to the park," she declared. "At least it will be cool there."

The ten of them trooped back to the parking lot. Mallory felt as if all they'd done since the trip had begun was load and unload kids from cars. But she was looking forward to the park. At least she'd be able to sit down and not worry about entertaining the kids. They were going to see the play *Hansel and Gretel*.

"Look at all these parking spaces!" Mrs. Barrett exclaimed as she pulled into the empty lot by the park's theater. "I'm going to take that as a good omen."

It wasn't. The deserted parking lot meant they were too early. The sign outside the box office said the performance would start at three o'clock. Over an hour to wait.

"What kind of a theater is this?" Mrs. Barrett said, shoving back the lock of hair that had fallen over one eye. "All matinees begin at two. Everyone knows that."

Franklin, who was trying to make the best of things, suggested they skip rocks across the pond. That sounded like a good idea, except for the fact that there were no stones within sight of the pond. The water's edge was swampy and Suzi and Madeleine promptly soaked their shoes and socks. They had to go barefoot till the play began.

Mallory and Franklin and Mrs. Barrett were relieved when it was time for the show to start. Unfortunately, ten minutes into the play, the witch appeared and frightened Marnie so badly that Mrs. Barrett had to take her out of the theatre.

After the play Franklin took his kids to his car while Mallory led Buddy and Suzi to Mrs. Barrett's car. Mrs. Barrett sat in the front seat with her forehead resting on the steering wheel. Marnie was in the back, asleep in her carseat.

"Ahem." Mallory cleared her throat loudly.

Mrs. Barrett lifted her head. Her eyes looked a little red, as if she had been crying. Mallory felt terrible for her. But before she could say a word, Franklin appeared at the car. He looked as exhausted and upset as Mrs. Barrett.

"Look, Natalie, I'm just going to take the kids on home. They're pretty wiped out. I'll call you later tonight."

Mrs. Barrett tried to smile. "That's fine,

Franklin. 'Bye!" Franklin walked away and Mrs. Barrett started her car. "Oh, Mallory," she said with a sigh. "I wanted this day to be perfect. And it's been a disaster. A complete disaster."

Mallory didn't know what to say. So she didn't say anything.

CHAPTER 6

W hile Mallory was baby-sitting for the Barretts, Jeff was at the Pike house visiting Mal's brothers. He sprang out of bed on Saturday morning and, after inhaling a piece of toast and a bowl of granola, raced out the back door.

"I'll be with the triplets all day," he called over his shoulder to Mom. "See you at dinner!"

Mary Anne and I watched him bicycle down the road from my bedroom window. "It's good to have Jeff home, isn't it?" Mary Anne said.

"Yup," I replied, flopping on my stomach on my bed. "Even if he did finish off the granola and take my bike without asking. I can't believe he'll be gone the entire day."

"That will give us time to concentrate on other things," Mary Anne said. "Like choosing our outfits for the family portrait."

"I hadn't even thought about that." I raised

myself onto one elbow. You're right, that is important.''

Mary Anne threw open the doors of my closet. "I've been thinking about wearing my pink dress with the drop waist. But if I wear that, then you really can't wear your new orange dress. We'd clash.''

I wrinkled my nose. "You're right, we would. What if I wear the pale lavender and you wear your navy blue? How would that look?''

"I don't know,'' Mary Anne said. "Let's try them on and see.''

Mary Anne went to her closet and hauled out every dress she'd bought in the past three years into my room. She dumped them on the bed in a big heap. I did the same. My room looked as if it had been hit by a tornado.

For the rest of the morning and part of the afternoon, Mary Anne and I tried on clothes. Then we fixed our hair and even polished our nails.

While we were having a fashion parade, Jeff was playing with the triplets. Since they hadn't written or talked for so long, they had a lot of catching up to do.

"Dad got me a really good boogie board,'' Jeff told them after they'd climbed several trees and wrestled. "Now I spend practically every weekend at the beach.''

"We go to Fun City Amusement Park as many times as we can," Adam said.

Byron nodded. "Our parents finally let us ride El Monstro."

"Last time we were there," Jordan added, "we rode that roller coaster ten times. It was a Pike record."

"Cool. Hey, you guys want to kick a soccer ball around?" Jeff asked.

"We don't have a soccer ball," Adam answered.

"You're kidding," Jeff said. "Everyone in California plays soccer."

"Not in Stoneybrook," Jordan said. "Baseball's our game."

"You want to play some ball?" Byron asked.

"Sure," Jeff replied. "Have you got a glove I can borrow?"

Jeff and the Pikes played ball until dinnertime. Mom had to call Jeff and remind him to come home.

"I'm starved," he announced as he threw open the front door. We were all waiting for him in the living room. "What's for dinner?"

"Enchiladas, tostadas, burritos, and salsa," Mom replied with a grin. "We're going to Casa Grande tonight."

"All right!" Jeff raised one fist in the air. "Mexican food is my favorite."

"I know," Mom said with a smile.

"And after that, we're going to a movie," I said. "They just re-did the Cineplex at Washington Mall and it's supposed to be really cool."

Mary Anne nodded in agreement. "It's huge. They show ten movies at once."

"Here's the newspaper." Richard handed the *Stoneybrook News* to Jeff. "As our guest of honor, you get to pick the movie."

Jeff spread the newspaper out on the living room rug. After about ten minutes of sighing and scratching his head, he said, "I think we should see *The Mutant From Outer Space*."

"You're making that up," Mom said. "That couldn't be a real movie."

"I'm serious. See?" Jeff turned the paper so Mom could read it. "The mutant destroyed one planet and now he's ready to ruin another."

"Do you really want to see that?" Richard asked, peering over his glasses.

Jeff folded his arms across his chest. "Definitely."

"All right!" Richard said. "The mutant it is."

Our dinner together was lots of fun. We devoured two baskets of chips and salsa at Casa Grande, then ate full dinners with fried ice cream for dessert. After that, we hurried over to the Cineplex to see *The Mutant From Outer Space*.

Except for three kids in the very front row, we were the only people in our theater. Even though we had just eaten an entire Mexican dinner, Jeff insisted on ordering buttered popcorn and Junior Mints.

"A movie's not a movie unless you have popcorn," he said.

Have you ever seen a movie that is so bad it's good? That's what *The Mutant From Outer Space* was like. The mutant had two heads that kept arguing with each other. One head would say, "I will kill everyone and take over this planet." Then the other head would say, "No, *I'm* going to kill everyone and take over the universe."

At first we watched quietly but by about halfway through the movie, we were laughing out loud at the parts that weren't even supposed to be funny.

Then Mom and Jeff started yelling right along with the characters in the movie, "It's the mutant. Run!"

Tears were running down Mary Anne's face and I nearly fell out of my seat laughing. After the movie was over, Mary Anne said, "That was one of my all time favorite movie experiences." And I think she meant it.

"Should we see it again?" Jeff asked.

"Noooo!" we bellowed.

"Once was more than enough," Richard added. "But I would like to see the sequel. What do you think they'll call it?"

"It'll be something like *Revenge of the Mutants*," Jeff said.

"Or *The Mutants Fight Back*," I said.

"Or *Son of the Mutant*," Mary Anne added.

An usher who overheard us talking said, "There actually is a sequel. And it's called *The Mutant From Outer Space Part Two*."

I don't know why that struck us as so funny. But we giggled all the way to the car. During the drive back to Stoneybrook we discussed our upcoming trip.

"I guess we better decide where to go," Mom said. "Is it Washington D. C. or Boston?"

"I've always loved Boston," Richard said. "Because of the clam chowder and the historic old sights. Faneuil Hall, Bunker Hill, the Freedom Trail."

"I think watching whales would be the absolute best," Jeff said, leaning forward in his seat.

"I heard the Sleepy Hollow Cemetery is good," I said. "And scary." If you haven't guessed, I love ghost stories, haunted houses, and anything that gives you goose bumps.

"I want to go to the Museum of Fine Arts,"

Mary Anne said. "It's supposed to have one of the best Egyptian collections in the world."

"Oooh!" Jeff turned to me. "You'd like that. All of those dead mummies wrapped in ace bandages."

"How about the Public Garden at Boston Common?" Richard asked.

"Yes!" We all cheered on that one.

Richard flicked the turn signal and guided the car into our driveway. He turned off the engine and smiled. "Well, I guess we've made our decision. We're going to Boston."

"All right!" Jeff cried. "Paul Revere, here we come."

That night, I got in bed and sighed contentedly. Jeff was home and we were having a fantastic time. I thought about how much I loved him and what fun we were going to have over the next week. I'm sure I fell asleep with a smile on my face.

Unfortunately, things started to go sour the very next morning. You see, Richard is pretty strict. Much more so than my mom or dad. He insists that beds are made before you leave the house and that dishes are washed immediately after meals. Jeff didn't understand that.

"Why can't we do the dishes later?" Jeff asked after we'd eaten a breakfast of waffles and strawberries. "I have to get over to the Pikes'."

"Cleaning up will only take a few minutes," Richard said. "That way we don't have to look at a sink full of dishes for half the day."

Jeff remained rooted in place. "Mrs. Bruen doesn't mind dishes sitting around. She's always telling me to go have fun while I'm still young."

"Who's Mrs. Bruen?" Richard asked.

"Dad's housekeeper."

"Well, she may feel that way," Richard said, shoving his chair back from the table and standing up. "But I don't. Now help your sisters clean up."

"Okay," Jeff grumbled. He carried his plate into the kitchen, then wiped the counters, but he didn't smile once. As soon as the sink was empty, Jeff stormed out the back door and marched over to the Pikes'. He was back within an hour.

I found him sitting on the front porch swing staring forlornly at the ground.

"What's the matter, Jeff?" I asked, slipping into the swing next to him.

"The triplets," he muttered. "They've changed."

"In what way?" I asked.

"They used to be fun and we used to like the same things. But they don't even play soccer. Can you believe it?"

"Well, soccer isn't everything, is it?" I

asked. "I mean, couldn't you guys play other games together?"

"I wanted to play Frisbee, but they couldn't. They were going over to Scott Danby's house."

"Who's that?" I asked.

Jeff dug the toe of his sneaker into the porch floorboards. "Some new friend of theirs."

"Why didn't you go to Scott's with them?"

"They didn't ask me. Maybe they don't want to play with me anymore."

I put my arm around Jeff's shoulders. "I'm sure that's not true. Things just change when people are apart."

"I know." Jeff shoved off with his foot and we swung for several minutes in silence. Then he said, "What am I going to do for the next three days? Everyone will be in school. Or at work."

"Richard will be home," I reminded Jeff. "He *wants* to spend time with you."

"Oh. Great."

Obviously Jeff was not happy about the idea at all.

CHAPTER 7

I came home from school on Monday and found Jeff sitting at the kitchen table, looking forlorn.

"What's the matter?" I asked.

He slumped down in his chair. "I'm bored."

"Didn't you and Richard do anything today?"

Jeff made a face. "He took me to some museum to see a bunch of old paintings."

At that moment Richard appeared at the back door. He was carrying a softball and a mitt. "Hey, Jeff!" he said. "How about a game of catch?"

Jeff pulled himself to his feet and shuffled out the door. "Sure."

I watched them from the window. It only took a few seconds for me to realize that Jeff was a much better player than Richard. After a funny baseball pitcher wind-up, Richard tossed the softball. The throw landed in the grass several feet in front of Jeff.

When Jeff tossed the ball, Richard tripped over the garden hose and sprawled flat on his back. He tried to make a joke of it, but I could tell he was really embarrassed.

I watched as they threw the ball back and forth for a few more minutes without too many misses. I could see that Jeff was trying to be nice to Richard and act like he was having a good time. But I knew he wasn't.

As I rode my bike to the Barretts', a knot was forming in my stomach. Jeff's visit wasn't going quite the way I'd hoped. But I didn't know how to fix it. And baby-sitting for the Barretts didn't make me feel any better. They were having their own troubles.

Mrs. Barrett needed a sitter for just an hour before the BSC meeting, so she could prepare the perfect dinner for Franklin. She met me at the front door wearing a frilly apron. She had slipped a cooking mitt on one hand and held a spatula in the other.

"The kids are in the living room waiting for you," she said. "Don't let them eat or drink anything or go outside. They're wearing their best outfits."

I found the children sitting on the couch looking like tiny dolls. The girls were dressed in matching blue and white polka dot dresses with anklets and black patent leather shoes.

Buddy was wearing blue pants, a white shirt, and a red bow tie. All of their faces were scrubbed shiny clean. They looked miserable.

"Don't touch anything," Buddy said to me. "Mom just polished the furniture. You might get fingerprints on it."

"Don't put your feet on the couch," Suzi added. "That's clean, too."

"It looks great," I said, spinning in a circle. Usually magazines are scattered across the coffee table, juice cups and unfinished crackers sit on the end tables, and toys cover every inch of the carpet, but not today. I barely recognized the place.

"Thanks," Mrs. Barrett called from the kitchen. "I've spent two days cleaning."

"What's the big occasion?" I asked.

"Franklin and his children are coming to dinner," Mrs. Barrett explained. "After last Saturday's disastrous outing, I wanted to make sure everything would be perfect. So I planned the menu in advance, set the table, and rented a movie for the kids to watch."

"What are you having for dinner?"

"Lasagna, garlic cheese sticks, a fresh broccoli and carrot medley, and spumoni ice cream."

"Wow." I couldn't believe what I was hearing. Mrs. Barrett is usually the microwave queen, cooking frozen macaroni and cheese dinners and hot dogs in four minutes. I don't think I'd ever seen her cook a full dinner.

"Franklin says Italian food is his kids favorite," she said, rubbing a smudge of tomato sauce off her face with the back of her hand. "I hope they like this."

"I'm sure they will," I replied, surveying the dining table. A vase of fresh flowers stood in the center of the table, surrounded by nine place mats with linen napkins in napkin rings. "Isn't this a lot of hard work just for one dinner?"

Mrs. Barrett blushed and smiled. "It's worth it. I think Franklin is very special."

"Mom!" Suzi called from the living room. "I really have to go to the bathroom. Can I?"

"Oh, dear," Mrs. Barrett whispered to me. "I told them to sit on the couch and not move a muscle. Now they're afraid to do anything."

"I'll get Suzi," I said to Mrs. Barrett. "You finish dinner."

"Thanks." Mrs. Barrett smiled. "I'm pretty much squared away in the kitchen. Now I have to choose the right outfit and fix my hair. Would you keep the kids occupied till Franklin gets here?"

"No sweat," I said. "I brought my Kid-Kit. There's enough stuff inside to keep them busy for hours."

While Mrs. Barrett hurried upstairs to change, I laid out supplies. I had scissors, crayons, and construction paper.

"I've got an idea," I said to the kids. "Why don't we make masks?"

"That sounds like fun," Buddy said.

"What should we make?" I asked.

"The Little Mermaid," Suzi cried.

"I want to be a dinosaur," Buddy said. "We better hurry," he added as he carefully drew a dinosaur head on a piece of paper. "Those kids are coming and they'll want to steal our masks."

"I don't think they'd do that," I said. "But they may want to play with them. You'll let them do that, won't you?"

Buddy stared at the carpet. "Well . . . maybe."

We spent the next hour coloring masks. At 5:20 I had to leave for the BSC meeting. Franklin hadn't arrived but Mrs. Barrett seemed to be as ready as she'd ever be.

"Good luck!" I called when I left for Claud's.

"Thanks," Mrs. Barrett replied. "I'll need it."

I rode my bike to Claudia's house and arrived with five minutes to spare. Everyone was there, chatting.

"Who wants treats?" Claudia asked, reaching for a bag of candy kisses that she'd stashed on her closet shelf. She passed the bag around and everyone took one except Stacey and me.

"How was Mrs. Barrett?" Mallory asked as she munched on her chocolate. "The last time I saw her she was really depressed."

"She's trying to be Suzie Homemaker," I said. "You should have seen her house. It was immaculate. And the kids looked like little dolls."

"Those aren't the Barretts I know," Kristy said.

"She's trying to impress Franklin," I told her. "But if you ask me, she's trying too hard."

Claudia flopped onto the bed. "Maybe they're in love."

"Well if they are, then Franklin should love her the way she is," Stacey pointed out, "and not expect her to be some perfect person that only exists on old TV shows."

"Yeah," Jessi giggled. "Like the mother on *Leave it to Beaver.*"

Mary Anne, who had been quiet, said, "I think I know what Mrs. Barrett's going through. The same thing is happening to my dad. He wants Jeff to like him and be his friend, but he doesn't know how to go about it."

"Taking him to boring museums and making him play catch is not the way to do it," I said.

Mary Anne looked confused. "But I thought Jeff liked to play sports."

"He does," I said. "But with someone who's athletic. You should see your dad with a ball and glove. He's a complete dork."

I didn't mean to hurt Mary Anne's feelings but I could tell by the look on her face that I had.

"Dad didn't *have* to take time off work," Mary Anne snapped. "He did it for Jeff. Maybe your brother would like to spend the next two days alone."

"I was just joking," I shot back. "Can't you take a joke?"

Mary Anne pursed her lips. "If that was a joke, it wasn't very funny."

The other members of the BSC sat staring at their hands, pretending not to notice that Mary Anne and I were having a little problem. Unfortunately our little problem was about to begin growing bigger.

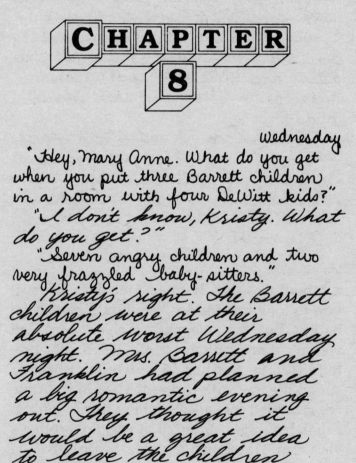

CHAPTER 8

Wednesday

"Hey, Mary Anne. What do you get when you put three Barrett children in a room with four DeWitt kids?"

"I don't know, Kristy. What do you get?"

"Seven angry children and two very frazzled baby-sitters."

Kristy's right. The Barrett children were at their absolute worst Wednesday night. Mrs. Barrett and Franklin had planned a big romantic evening out. They thought it would be a great idea to leave the children together.

Wrong.

anyway, they were
barely out the door when
the Barretts started
throwing food and calling
the DeWitt kids names.
  Well, the DeWitt children weren't
any better, Mary Anne. I watched the
oldest one deliberately spill Marnie's
milk on the floor and then blame
Buddy.
  Let's face it. Sitting for
them was like playing
referee to the War of the
Worlds. I never want to
do that again.
  Me neither.

School was out. We had four days of vacation to look forward to. We should have been
happy but we weren't. Richard and Jeff
weren't getting along at all. Jeff finally pretended to be sick just so he wouldn't have to
spend the day with Richard. Then Mary Anne
criticized Jeff for canceling her father's outing.
I took Jeff's side. After all, it was my brother's
vacation. He should be able to do what he
wanted. Mary Anne said Jeff hurt her father's
feelings. A crack was starting to form in our
family.

Things didn't seem much better at the Barretts' house. After the BSC meeting on Wednesday, Mary Anne and Kristy grabbed their Kid-Kits and bicycled over there to babysit. (Two sitters were needed, because there were seven kids at the house.) The DeWitt kids had already arrived and were sitting shoulder to shoulder on the couch. Directly across from them, with arms folded firmly across their chests, were Buddy, Suzi, and Marnie.

"It looks like a war zone," Kristy whispered to Mary Anne.

Mary Anne nodded. "I have a feeling we're in for a very long evening."

And she was right. Dinner launched the battle between the two families.

"Mrs. Barrett put frozen pizzas in the oven for dinner," Mary Anne announced after the adults had driven away.

"What kind of pizza?" Madeleine asked.

"It looks like Super Deluxe Combos," Kristy called from the kitchen. "That's pepperoni and sausage, onions, green peppers, and olives."

"I hate onions," Taylor said, wrinkling his nose. "Can you take them off?"

"I like them," Buddy shot back. "Leave them on."

"I'm not eating anything that has touched olives," Lindsey added. "Let's put on extra cheese instead. That's what we do at our house."

"Well at *our* house we put on pineapple," Suzi said, in her most haughty voice. "So there."

"This sounds like a conversation my family might have," Mary Anne murmured to Kristy. "Dawn and Jeff are the pickiest eaters on the earth. No matter what Dad or I make, they have to change it."

"I want a burger," Ryan, the youngest DeWitt, suddenly announced.

His sisters and brother took this as an opportunity to show a united front. "We want hamburgers," Lindsey started chanting. "We want hamburgers."

You can't outshout a Barrett kid. And to prove it, Buddy stood on his chair and bellowed, "Pizza! Pizza! We want pizza!"

Can you imagine seven children shouting at once? It was so loud that Mary Anne had to cover her ears. Kristy had been to a Krusher practice that afternoon and was still wearing her whistle around her neck. She put the whistle in her mouth and blew.

TWEET!

Everyone stopped shouting at once.

"All right," Kristy barked in her coach voice. "Listen up. There will be no more shouting this evening. I'm sorry if you don't like pizza, but that's what's for dinner. You can pick the food you don't like off your slice and put it on your plate. Is that clear?"

Everyone nodded.

"Good." Kristy looked at Mary Anne to see if she wanted to say anything.

"Let's go sit at the dinner table," Mary Anne said. "I think it would be fun for each Barrett to sit next to a DeWitt. That way you can all get to know each other better."

Mary Anne's idea seemed like a good one, but it soon became clear that the children didn't *want* to know each other better.

"Get your elbow off my spot," Lindsey said to Marnie who was happily munching on a pizza crust.

"Don't yell at my sister, pizza face," Buddy barked at Lindsey.

Taylor, who was sitting across from them, hurled a piece of pepperoni at Buddy. It hit him in the shoulder. "You leave my sister alone, jerk!"

"You're the jerk." Buddy threw his entire slice of pizza back at Taylor. Luckily it didn't hit him. Instead it flopped facedown on the kitchen floor. Ryan and Marnie saw the angry looks on their brothers' faces and burst into tears.

"Time out!" Kristy put her hands together in a T formation. "Food fighting is absolutely forbidden. So is name-calling. Now everybody, face forward and finish your dinner."

The kids ate the rest of the meal in silence. Several times, Mary Anne caught Buddy sticking his tongue out at Taylor. And once she saw Madeleine and Suzi kicking each other under the table.

After dinner, Mary Anne and Kristy led them into the rec room. Mary Anne had packed the game Candy Land in her Kid-Kit but changed her mind about suggesting they play it.

"I don't think they can handle playing a game together," she whispered to Kristy.

Kristy nodded. "We better give them an activity they can do on their own. I brought Play-Doh and cookie cutters in my kit. Let's try that."

Buddy helped Mary Anne spread newspaper out on the rec room floor while Kristy set out her cans of Play-Doh. There were four of them — one red, one yellow, a blue, and a green. Of course, they all wanted to use the same color.

Suzi grabbed the blue can first. "Mine!"

"Give me that!" Lindsey ordered. "That's my favorite color."

"No, you can't have it," Suzi said, stubbornly holding onto the can.

"I want blue, too," Taylor said, trying to pry it out of Suzi's arms.

"No!" Suzi bellowed.

"Suzi!" Taylor gasped and pointed. "Look behind you. There's a monster."

"Where?" Suzi dropped the can and looked over her shoulder.

"Ah ha!" Taylor snatched up the Play-Doh and grinned wickedly. "Now I've got the blue. And no one else can have it."

"Waaaaah!" Suzi burst into tears.

Mary Anne and Kristy decided things were reaching a crisis point. They had a quick huddle and made a decision.

"I really hate to do this," Mary Anne said to the kids, "but we're going to have to separate you. Barretts, please come upstairs with me."

"And I'll stay with the rest of you in the rec room," Kristy said to the DeWitts. "I've got coloring books and crayons in my Kid-Kit. I want you to play quietly until your father gets back."

The DeWitts gulped and exchanged we're-going-to-get-in-trouble looks. But Kristy and Mary Anne were more concerned about why they were misbehaving.

"The kids seem angry and scared," Kristy said as they rode their bikes to my house that night.

"What do they have to be scared of?" Mary Anne asked.

"I think they're worried that their parents will get married and they'll be lost in the shuffle," Kristy replied. "I know I felt that way when Mom married Watson."

"That's probably why Buddy was calling everyone names," Mary Anne said.

Kristy nodded. "If Mrs. Barrett marries Franklin, Buddy will suddenly have four stepbrothers and sisters. That's a lot."

"I know." Mary Anne sighed. "I've only got Dawn and Jeff, but that seems like two too many."

"Aren't you guys getting along?" Kristy asked.

Mary Anne shook her head. "No. Jeff is acting like a spoiled baby. Just because he's on vacation he thinks he can order us around. He never helps clean up unless he's forced to and worse, Dawn sticks up for him."

"Have you talked to Dawn about it?"

"If I say the least little thing about Jeff, Dawn has to top it by making some mean remark about Dad's lack of athletic ability."

"That doesn't sound good," Kristy said.

"It isn't. And here's the worst part — we're leaving on our trip tomorrow morning." Mary Anne's eyes started to fill with tears. "I don't know how we'll survive it."

CHAPTER 9

"I see Jeff's been here," Mary Anne said as she stepped through the front door Wednesday evening. She pointed to the jacket lying on the floor by the front closet. "I suppose he thinks the maid will hang up his clothes."

Mary Anne is not usually that snippy but baby-sitting for the Barrett and DeWitt kids had put her in a bad mood.

"He just forgot to hang it up," I replied. "He must have been in a hurry."

"Yeah. A hurry to get away from my father. Which I don't appreciate one single bit."

There was something about her tone that made me angry. "Well, for your information," I snapped back, "your father is ruining my brother's vacation."

Mary Anne looked like she'd been slapped. Her eyes widened and her cheeks turned

75

bright red. She turned on her heel and rushed upstairs to her bedroom.

Slam!

Mom stuck her head in the hall when she heard Mary Anne's door bang shut. "What was all that about?"

I decided not to tell Mom about my fight with Mary Anne. (I was already feeling bad for what I'd said about Richard.) I just muttered, "Mary Anne had a rough time babysitting."

"I hope you kids are packed because Richard plans to leave bright and early tomorrow morning."

I wasn't packed. I trudged up the stairs to my room. I could just imagine what our trip would be like. Everyone would be snapping at each other.

I paused outside of Mary Anne's door. I could hear her slamming around inside her room. She was obviously still angry. I went into my room and locked the door. (If she was going to shut me out, I'd do the same to her!)

I took my suitcase out from under my bed and put in two pairs of shorts (in case it was hot), two dresses (in case we went someplace nice for dinner), a pair of jeans (to wear in the park and whale watching), several tops (to go with the jeans and shorts), and a windbreaker (in case it got cold). I made sure to pack plenty of underwear and socks. Then I picked jewelry to go with my outfits. I could barely fit everything in my suitcase. I had to sit on the lid to close it.

Packing took about an hour. When I'd finished, I stuck my head into the hallway. Mary Anne's door was still closed.

I crossed the hall and tapped lightly on it. "Mary Anne?"

No answer.

I put my ear to the door. I heard rustling sounds. Mary Anne was in her room. And she was ignoring me.

"Go ahead. Be anti-social!" I yelled through the door. "See if I care."

I waited. Not a peep of a reply.

"Oh, brother," I muttered as I walked back to my own room. "Some vacation this is going to be."

That night, I barely got any sleep. I felt bad that Mary Anne and I had gone to bed without making up and I tossed and turned for hours. I didn't feel any better when Richard pounded on my bedroom door at five A.M. Nobody in his right mind gets up that early.

"Rise and shine! Rise and shine!" he sang cheerily. "The Spier limousine will be leaving in twenty minutes."

Then he flicked my light switch on and off. (Which I absolutely hate.) I pulled my pillow over my head and growled, "Why do we have to leave so early? It's still dark out."

Richard pulled my pillow off my head and said, "If we leave now we'll arrive just in time for lunch. Then we can sightsee all afternoon."

"I can't wait," I groaned.

Mary Anne and I passed each other in the hall on the way to the shower. "Good morning," Mary Anne said stiffly.

"Good morning," I answered. Mary Anne and I never say that to each other. But now we were being extra-polite as if we were people in a motel who didn't know each other.

Jeff hates getting up early (even more than I do). So he was in an extra-foul mood. He sulked through breakfast, barely touching his granola, and then refused to help pack the car. Jeff sat on the front steps and watched as the rest of us loaded the suitcases, the cooler, the picnic basket, and cameras into the car. When we finally decided who got to sit by the windows (Jeff and Mary Anne), my brother made an announcement.

"I want to go to Washington D.C.," he said.

"What?!" Mom gasped. "But I thought you wanted to see Boston."

Jeff stuck out his lower lip in a pout. "I've changed my mind. We have to go to Washington."

Mom and Richard exchanged concerned looks and then she said, "I'm sorry, Jeff, but we've already made hotel reservations."

"Cancel them!"

"We can't," Richard replied. "At least not without losing our deposit."

"Mom!" Jeff whined. "You said we could go to Washington if we wanted to! Well, I want to and so does Dawn." He turned to me for support. "Don't you?"

I was perfectly willing to take my brother's side in a lot of things, but even I knew this was an unreasonable request. "Look, Jeff, we agreed on Boston. Don't you want to go whale watching and see the big ships?"

Jeff didn't answer. Instead he slumped down in his seat and turned his head to stare out the window. It was terrible. I had my brother, who wasn't speaking to me, on one side and Mary Anne, who was being overly polite, on the other.

"How about singing a song?" Mom suggested as we drove out of Stoneybrook.

"All right," I said, trying to sound cheery. "What song?"

"Does everybody know 'The Happy Wanderer'?" Richard asked, looking at me in the rearview mirror.

" 'The Happy Wanderer'?" I heard Jeff snort under his breath. "What a goon."

"I don't know it," I said. "Think of another."

"There's always 'Oh, Susannah,' " Mom said.

"All righty," I replied, trying to sound enthusiastic.

The singalong was a bust. Mom, Richard, and I sang while Mary Anne and Jeff sat silently. I think Mary Anne refused to sing because my mom had thought of the idea.

When Richard suggested we play "I'm going on a trip," she really perked up.

"That's a good idea, Dad," Mary Anne said sweetly.

"Instead of saying, 'I'm going on a trip'," he added, "We could say, 'I'm going to Boston.' "

"That sounds fun," Mom said. "Mary Anne, why don't you start?"

"I'm going on a trip" is a pretty easy game to play. The players take turns telling what they're going to take in their suitcases, but they have to list things in alphabetical order. Mary Anne started with A.

"I'm going on a trip to Boston," Mary Anne said. "And I'm taking an aardvark."

Richard chuckled extra-loudly at that one. On another day, I might have laughed, too, but I didn't find it very funny this time.

"All right, Dawn." Mom shot me a pleading look that meant, "Please be nice" and then added, "It's your turn."

I sat up straight and forced a cheery smile. "Okay. I'm going on a trip to Boston and I'm going to take an aardvark and a baboon."

"Jeff?" Mom tapped him on the knee. "You're up."

Jeff's forehead was still resting against the window. He stayed in that position and mumbled, "If I were going on a trip to *Washington D.C.*, I'd take an aardvark, a baboon, and a baseball."

"That's not the way the game is played," Mary Anne said, leaning across me. "You're supposed to take something that starts with the letter C."

"I didn't know that," Jeff said.

"I think you *did* know that," Mary Anne told him. "You just screwed up the game to be a pest."

I had been irritated with Jeff myself, but what Mary Anne said made me mad. "You and your father may have played this game before," I explained tensely, "But Jeff hasn't. So don't call him a liar."

"I didn't call him a liar," she hissed. "I called him a pest. Which he is."

That did it. I didn't want to have anything to do with Mary Anne for the rest of the car ride. When we stopped for gas in Providence, I bought a bunch of postcards and spent the rest of the car trip writing to my friends.

Thursday-On the Road

Dear Stacey,

Well, the Spiers and the Schafers are on our way to Boston. We <u>had</u> planned to have a good time but I don't think that's going to happen. Mary Anne and Richard are ruining everything. First Mary Anne refused to join the singalong because it was Mom's idea. Then she started calling Jeff names. Then her dad made us play this really stupid car game. Only two days, 8 hours and fifty-three minutes till we get back to Stoneybrook. I can't wait!

Love, Dawn

CHAPTER 10

Thursday- at the Parker House Hotel

Dear Kristy,
  Some vacation! We were nearly killed crossing the Harvard Bridge into Boston. Mom and Richard were discussing which turn to take to get to our hotel, when a taxi swerved into our lane. We missed him by a half inch. Mary Anne said it was Mom's fault for talking to her dad while he was trying to drive. I said it was Richard's fault for not listening to Mom.

Now Mary Anne isn't speaking to me. Only two days, 7 hours, and forty-two minutes till we see good old Stoneybrook again. I'm counting the minutes.

Love, Dawn

Mom and Richard had booked two rooms at the Parker House. One for them and one for Mary Anne and Jeff and me. But Mary Anne refused to stay with us. Can you believe it? She said Jeff and I were acting too childish.

"I'd really rather stay with the adults," she said as she carried her suitcase through the door that joined the two bedrooms.

"Well, we're glad you're not staying here," I called after her, "because two's company and three's a *crowd*!"

"Yeah, Mary Anne," Jeff chimed in. "You're the one acting like a baby. Running to your dad."

Mary Anne stuck her tongue out at us and then shut the door.

I turned to Jeff and said in an extra-loud voice. "I'm glad Mary Anne's not staying with us. She's such a party pooper."

"Now we can have some real fun." Jeff moved to the window and peered down at the street below. The Parker House has fourteen floors and we were on the eighth. "I wish we had water balloons. It would be fun to throw them on people."

"It's too bad," I said, sounding as if I agreed with Jeff. But I didn't. Water balloons can hurt. At that distance, it would be like dropping a big rock on someone's head.

"Hey, I got it," Jeff snapped his fingers. "Let's call room service and order something gross like brains and eggs and have them deliver it to Mary Anne."

I hated to admit it, but Jeff was sounding just a little bit childish. I tried to discourage him. "Mary Anne would know it was us. We need to think of a really creative way to get her. But it should be *outside* the hotel."

Jeff started listing ways that we could get rid of Mary Anne. "How about shoving her on a bus. To China."

"I don't think buses go there," I pointed out. "You'd need to take a boat."

"A boat!" he cried. "That's even better. We'll put her on one of those big sailing ships in Boston Harbor. It'd be years before we ever saw her again."

Knock, knock.

"It's her," Jeff whispered.

"She's probably going to tell us that the adults are boring and she wants to come back to our room."

"But we won't let her," Jeff said with a sly smile.

"Right." I agreed with Jeff. Mary Anne was the one who had walked out on us. "She'll just have to suffer."

I glared at the door and called, "Come in."

To my surprise, it wasn't Mary Anne, but her dad who stuck his head through the door.

"Ready to be tourists?" Richard asked.

Jeff flopped on the bed, looking extra-bored. "I guess. If we have to."

"Good." Richard ignored Jeff's behavior. "Then we'll begin at the Freedom Trail."

Jeff sat up. "I thought we were going to see Boston, not some trail through the woods."

Richard chuckled and shoved his glasses up on his nose with one finger. "The Freedom Trail is a walking tour of Boston's historical sights."

"You mean like museums?" Jeff had seen enough of those in Stoneybrook.

"Yes, there are museums," Richard said, "but the Freedom Trail is more than that. It's like traveling back through time. Back to the moment when our forefathers first broke away from England and formed a new country. We'll visit the Old South Meeting House where the colonists met to plan the rebellion called the Boston Tea Party. We'll visit Faneuil Hall, and discover why it's called the Cradle of Liberty. We'll tour Paul Revere's house. That's where he was living when he took the midnight ride crying, 'The British are coming! The British are coming!' "

"Richard, you sound so excited," I said, chuckling. "They should hire you to make a TV commercial for Boston."

"I can't help it," Richard said. "Boston's one of my favorite cities."

"Why is it called the Freedom *Trail*? Is it made of dirt?" Jeff asked.

Richard smiled mysteriously. "Let's go see."

Mary Anne and Mom had changed into their walking shoes and were waiting for us in the hall. Mom said hello, but Mary Anne was silent. We took the elevator down to the lobby and then hurried out onto the street.

Richard gestured grandly for us to stand still. Then he said, "The first stop on our tour is the Parker House Hotel."

"Our hotel?" I asked.

"That's right. Turn around and take a look at the nation's oldest hotel in continuous operation. Among some of its most noteworthy guests were Charles Dickens and John Wilkes Booth."

"The guy who assassinated Lincoln?" Jeff asked. He stood looking up at the building for several seconds and then said, "I wonder if he stayed in our room."

"I hope not," I said with a shudder. "I'd much prefer Charles Dickens."

Mom led us across the street to our next stop on the Freedom Trail. It was a marble building with six pillars across the front and a square tower on top. "This is King's Chapel," Mom announced. "The first Unitarian church in America."

Richard, who was studying one of the numerous books that he had crammed into his pocket, said, "It is also the first church designed by mail order plans. Oh! And look at this." Richard stepped up to one of the pillars and knocked on it. "This pillar is made out of wood and painted to look like marble."

That impressed all of us. We each took turns saying, "Knock on wood!" and rapping our knuckles against the pillars.

The burial ground next to King's Chapel was surrounded by a low black iron fence. "Dawn, this should interest you," Richard read from his guide book. "This burying ground is the oldest in the city."

"Look at that weird gravestone," Jeff said,

pointing at something between two of the marble tombstones.

Mary Anne rolled her eyes at Jeff. "That's not a gravestone, silly. That's a ventilator shaft for the 'T' — Boston's subway."

"Oh." Jeff stared at the ground, embarrassed. Mary Anne didn't have to act like Ms. Know-it-All and make Jeff feel dumb. That must have hurt his feelings.

"What's next, Mom?" I asked, linking my arm through my mother's and Jeff's. "We're ready to leave."

"Just follow the red brick road," Mom said. Mom pointed to the red stripe on the sidewalk. "That's the trail."

Jeff and I ducked our heads down and followed the stripe to the next stop. "Here's a statue of Ben Franklin," I said pointing to a huge bronze statue in front of Old City Hall. "And some other guy."

"That other guy," Richard said as he followed us with his nose still in the guidebook, "is Josiah Quincy."

"Never heard of him," Jeff said.

"He was the second mayor of the city. They named Quincy Market after him," Richard explained.

Mary Anne, who had her own guidebook (like father, like daughter), said, "Ben Franklin's statue is standing where Boston's very first school used to be." She spun around to look behind her. "The building was later moved across the street. But it says in this book that people like John Hancock actually studied here. Wow."

Jeff shook his head. "I didn't know those guys even went to school."

Mom laughed and ruffled his hair. "Schools have been around since the beginning of time."

"Too bad," Jeff cracked.

"Look, Dad," Mary Anne pointed to the red brick cottage with the bay windows that sat on the corner of School and Washington streets. "There's The Old Corner Bookstore. Every author who was anybody used to hang out there."

Mom nodded. "Longfellow, Emerson, Hawthorne, Holmes — "

"Sherlock Holmes was here?" Jeff asked.

"No, silly," Mary Anne said, rolling her eyes again. "*Oliver Wendell* Holmes. Sherlock Holmes is a made-up character."

I was tired of Mary Anne's attitude. "The only thing that makes you smart is that guidebook," I hissed at Mary Anne. "So quit acting like a know-it-all and quit picking on my brother."

Mary Anne's lower lip quivered. For a moment I thought she might cry.

Richard stepped between us. "Girls. There's no need to fight. We're all just a little tired. What we need is a nice refreshing glass of lemonade."

The cool drink did help. Richard bought them from a street vendor with a red wagon under a striped green umbrella. We were in a small park area directly in front of the Old South Meeting House. We sat on wooden benches and sipped our lemonade while Richard continued his history lesson.

"This is the place," Richard said, gesturing at the red brick church with the white steeple, "where the townspeople met and planned the famous, or I guess I should say, infamous, Boston Tea Party."

Now here's what floored me. For the first time, Mary Anne admitted that she didn't know what something was. "Was it an actual party?" she asked.

"No." Richard laughed. "It was more of a raid. The people were so upset about the new British tax on tea that they held a meeting to discuss the problem. Afterward, a lot of them dressed up like Indians and boarded the three big ships sitting in the harbor. The ships held huge cargo loads of tea which the Bostonians dumped in the harbor."

"Boy, I bet that made the British mad," I said.

Mom nodded. "They were so mad that they closed the port. Nothing could come in or go out."

By this time we'd finished our drinks and were ready to move on. Mary Anne and I hadn't even looked at each other since our argument by the bookstore. We certainly weren't talking to each other. We just talked to our parents.

"Mom," I said, standing up and stretching, "where to next?"

Richard, who was examining his map for the millionth time, said, "It looks like our next stop is the Old State House where Bostonians first heard the Declaration of Independence."

We passed the Old State House, pausing to look at the circle of cobblestones which mark the site where the Boston Massacre happened in 1770. Then we moved on to Faneuil Hall. Now you'd never know how to pronounce Faneuil just by looking at it on paper. We spotted a tour guide leading a group from a blue trolley car across the bricks to the Marketplace. Mom asked him how to pronounce the name. Are you ready? Fan-*yoo-ell*.

Anyway, Fan-*yoo-ell* Hall Marketplace is amazing. It's this huge marketplace packed with people and street performers and flower

92

vendors. We saw three guys juggling flaming batons and a couple of mimes pretending to be wind-up toys. There was even a guy playing the bagpipes dressed in a kilt. Across from Faneuil Hall is Quincy Market which has every kind of food stall you can imagine.

The first floor of Faneuil Hall has always been a market with all sorts of shops. The top half of it is used to be a meeting hall where orators and statesmen would meet.

"It's called the Cradle of Liberty," Richard explained to us as we shuffled through the crowded square toward the entrance, "because this is where the first protests against the British were voiced."

Richard wanted to talk more about the history, but I couldn't wait to go shopping. (I brought along every penny I'd saved from baby-sitting.)

Mary Anne said she wanted to tour the upstairs part of Faneuil Hall with Richard. Mom said she'd take Jeff and me through the marketplace. So we agreed to pick up food at Quincy Market (there are more than thirty-nine food stalls selling everything from exotic teas and cheese to baked beans) and then have a picnic dinner across the street in Waterfront Park.

When Richard and Mary Anne had left, Jeff turned to me with a big grin on his face and whispered, "Yea, it's just the Schafers. Alone at last."

Thursday night— 10 PM back at
                   the hotel
Dear Claud,
    Mom and Jeff and I shopped till we dropped today. It was great. I found souvenirs for every member of the BSC. Afterward we ate dinner at Waterfront Park with "silent" Mary Anne (she's barely speaking to me) and Richard. Then we went to a movie. (I sat in the middle row, she sat in the back.) Then we returned to our rooms. (Mary Anne's staying with Mom and Richard and I'm glad.) Only one day and 18 hours to go.
                    Love, Dawn
P.S. Don't eat too much junk food while I'm gone.

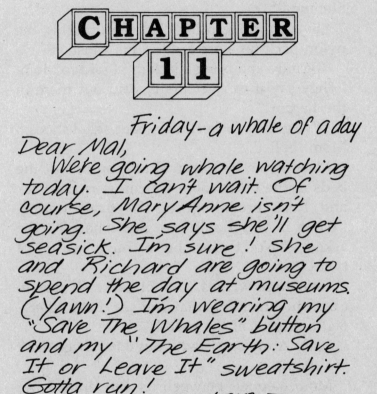

CHAPTER 11

Friday - a whale of a day

Dear Mal,
    We're going whale watching today. I can't wait. Of course, MaryAnne isn't going. She says she'll get seasick. I'm sure! She and Richard are going to spend the day at museums. (Yawn!) I'm wearing my "Save The Whales" button and my "The Earth: Save It or Leave It" sweatshirt. Gotta run!
                    Love, Dawn

"Jeff!" Mom called from her bedroom. "Make sure we have extra film for the camera. This is going to be the photo opportunity of a lifetime."

"I've got three rolls," Jeff said, patting the nylon pack he wore around his waist.

"Be sure and bring a jacket," I said to Mom. "They say it can get pretty cold out there in the harbor."

"I've got my jacket and rubber-soled shoes," Mom replied.

Mary Anne had been sitting on one of the beds in the other room watching us run back and forth preparing for the day's outing. "What if you don't see any whales?" she asked. "Won't that be a huge waste of time?"

"We'll see whales," I shot back. "It says in all of the brochures that you see them ninety-eight percent of the time."

Mary Anne persisted. "But what if you *don't* see them?"

Mom stepped between us and draped her arm across my shoulder. "Then we'll have had a very pleasant cruise together. Are you sure you don't want to come?"

Mary Anne folded her arms across her chest. "Positive. Dad and I are going to the Museum of Fine Arts this morning. Then we're going to have lunch at the Bostonian Hotel and visit the Boston Tea Party Museum."

"That sounds lovely," Mom said as Richard came into the room. She smiled and added, "I wish I could join you."

Jeff slipped his windbreaker on and said, "That's okay, Mom. Museums are for wimps."

Mom shot Jeff a stern look. "That's not true, Jeff, and you know it."

Jeff looked hurt. I could tell he expected Mom to take his side. But she wouldn't side with anyone. Neither would Richard.

"We landlubbers will meet you in the lobby after you get back," Richard said. "Let's synchronize our watches. Then you can tell us about your whale adventure and we'll tell you about the museums."

"I can't wait," Jeff muttered under his breath.

I jabbed him in the ribs. Richard was just trying to be nice and make Mom happy. Jeff didn't have to be so surly all the time.

We rode the elevator to the lobby together, but only Mom and Richard spoke to each other. Then we split up outside the hotel. Mom, Jeff, and I headed for Central Wharf.

A crowd of people were waiting at the pier when we arrived. A lot of them were clutching cups of hot coffee and holding coats and blankets in their arms. It gets cold out on the ocean!

The *Queen of Nantucket* looks like a big ferryboat. It has an upper and a lower deck. The lower deck is only six feet above the water line. You can almost put your hand in the water. When it was time to board, Jeff raced up the gangplank and grabbed a bench for us on the upper deck.

"We'll be heading west by northwest to the whales' feeding grounds," our guide's voice said over the intercom. "It's called Jeffrey's Ledge."

"Dawn!" Jeff exclaimed. "Did you hear that? The whales are having breakfast at my ledge."

"They also gather on Stellwagen Bank," the guide continued. "The bank is shallow — approximately one hundred fifty feet deep. Sediment from Massachusetts enriches the ocean floor and makes it an excellent breeding ground for plankton and plant life. This is a perfect time to be whale-watching, folks. I feel confident that we'll see quite a few of our ocean friends today."

It took about an hour and a half to reach Jeffrey's Ledge. In that time, Jeff and I explored every inch of the ship. We visited the captain's cabin, the cafeteria and snack bar, and browsed through the gift shop, which had a distinct whale theme. I saw rubber whales for the bathtub, whale T-shirts, whale hats, whale posters, and whale books. We decided to wait to buy anything until we'd actually seen a whale.

We didn't have long to wait.

"I see one!" was the cry that came from above. Suddenly everyone was shouting at once. "There are two. No, three!"

Jeff and I ran to the lower deck. We wanted to be close to the whales. Suddenly, one of them leapt out of the water. It was a humpback whale about fifty feet long. Can you imagine? That's as big as a school bus. It was gray and black with little white spots on its body and grooves that extended from the tip of its long snout down the center of its stomach. Water shot high in the air as it dove into the ocean.

"Look over there!" Jeff cried. "It's just a tail. He looks like he's dancing."

Jeff was right. The humpback must have been standing on his head as he slapped the water from side to side with what is called his fluke.

By this time Mom had joined us on the lower deck. "Isn't this thrilling?" she cried, as another whale leapt in the air. "They play almost like dolphins."

It was true. For such huge mammals, they seemed awfully active. We were enjoying watching them play until the one who had been standing on his head suddenly made a beeline for our boat. He looked like a giant torpedo cruising through the water.

"Mom, he's going to hit us!" I cried. "What'll we do?"

Mom clutched our arms and pulled us toward the wall of the ship. "Brace yourselves!"

At the last minute, the whale turned and nudged the side of the boat with a soft thud. You'll never guess what happened next. The whale rolled onto its side and began scratching his back against the hull of the boat. Isn't that fantastic?

After we'd bought souvenirs and postcards from the boat's gift shop, we rode the ferry back to Boston. What a great morning!

Friday- Boston Harbor
Dear Claudia,
     I'm in love. (With a humpback whale.) We whale watched all morning and I loved every second of it. But here's the weird thing. Even though Mary Anne and I aren't speaking, I kind of missed her. Every time a whale leapt out of the water, I thought, I wish Mary Anne were here. She'd really

like this. But she had to be stubborn and go to the museums with her dad! Well, it's her loss. See you in 1 day and six hours.

Dawn

On our way home from the wharf, we found a cute little vegetarian restaurant called Say Cheese! and ate lunch. Then we hurried to meet Mary Anne and Richard. They were in the lobby waiting for us.

"Well," Richard said with a big smile, "did you see a whale?"

"We saw a whole pod of whales," Jeff answered. "It was fantastic!"

"Oh, Richard," Mom said, "they were magnificent. I wish you could have seen them."

"I do, too." I could tell by the look on Richard's face that he really was disappointed that he had missed the whale-watching trip. "But we had a good time," he said, smiling at Mary Anne. "Didn't we, honey?"

"We could have spent all day at the Museum of Fine Arts' Egyptian collection," Mary Anne said. "But I loved seeing the Impressionist paintings. They have forty-three Monets."

"It sounds heavenly." Mom sighed. I realized that she wished she'd had a chance to go to the Museum of Fine Arts.

Mom and Richard exchanged sad looks. "Oh, well. Next time," Mom murmured.

"Now on to the rest of the day." Richard clapped his hands together. "What do you say we go to the New England Aquarium?"

"Yes!" all of us but Jeff cried.

"I don't want to go there," he said.

"Why not?" Mom asked. "It's the number-one attraction in the city. A must see."

"Listen to this, Jeff." Richard pulled a brochure out of his pocket and read, " 'The New England Aquarium has the largest cylindrical saltwater tank in the world. It is four stories high.' "

"Wow," I gasped, looking at Jeff. He didn't seem impressed.

Richard continued reading, " 'There are over seven thousand specimens and five times a day, divers go into the tank for feedings.' "

"There are also dolphin and sea lion shows," I added, remembering that Jeff usually likes that sort of thing.

Jeff shrugged. "We saw seals playing outside the aquarium when we left Central Wharf. I don't need to see them again."

"Oh, come on, Jeff," Mom pleaded. "The aquarium is supposed to be spectacular. I know you'll love it."

"Mom," Jeff whined. "We just spent five hours on the ocean. I don't feel like looking at any more fish or water."

Mom and I really wanted to go to the aquarium, but we couldn't leave Jeff. And I didn't feel comfortable going with Richard and Mary Anne. So Jeff, Mom, and I wound up at the Museum of Science.

Friday Afternoon—Science Park

Dear Jessi,

The Museum of Science is amazing. It has over four hundred exhibits including The Transparent Woman whose organs light up as they're described. The Omnimax Theatre is this giant domed screen that absolutely surrounds you with pictures and sound. Jeff loved it. So did I. Mary Anne wasn't with us. She and Richard went to the aquarium. It's like we're taking two separate vacations. Weird. One day and 3 hours to go.

Love, Dawn

Back at the hotel that night, we met for dinner but couldn't agree on anything.

"Should we try some Middle Eastern food?" Mom asked as we changed our clothes.

"That sounds good," I said.

"I feel like Chinese food," Mary Anne said.

Richard's face brightened. "I could go for Chinese. Chow mein, egg rolls, and that other stuff, moo goo something."

"Moo goo gai pan." Mom giggled. "We can go to a place called The Imperial Palace. It's in the heart of Chinatown."

"Okay," I said. "Sounds good to me."

"I don't feel like it," Jeff said, flopping on the bed. "We've been running around all day and I'm tired. Let's just stay at the hotel and order room service."

We all stared at Jeff for several moments before anyone spoke. Finally Mom asked, "Jeff? Are you really that tired?"

"I'm beat," Jeff murmured. "Please, Mom? Let's just stay here."

Mom pursed her lips and turned to Richard, who looked awfully tense. I could see a small muscle twitching in his jaw.

"Richard," Mom said. "I'm sorry. I better stay with Jeff. You take the girls and have fun."

I would much rather have gone to Chinatown, but I felt I should stay with Mom. So I said, "I guess I'm a little tired, too. I'll just stay here."

After Richard and Mary Anne left, Jeff got the room service menu that stood on the dressing table and made a big show of making up his mind about what to order.

"I think I'll have the shrimp cocktail," he said, putting on a British accent. "A small dinner salad. A large soup. A twice baked potato and broccoli florets." Then he turned to me and said, "That's just the appetizer. Now for the main course . . ."

I hit him with a nearby pillow and he retaliated by swatting at me with the menu. As we were goofing around I caught sight of Mom's reflection in the mirror. She was sitting on the edge of the other bed staring straight ahead, her hands clasped tightly in her lap. She looked as if she were about to cry. I felt terrible.

Friday night - Room 817

Dear Kristy,

Our vacation is like the Barretts vs. the DeWitts all over again. We've been separated since this morning. Right now, Mary Anne and Richard are in Chinatown eating dinner. Jeff and I ordered lasagna and salads from room service. Mom didn't eat anything. She was too upset. It's a good thing there's less than 24 hours to go. See you in Stoney brook.

Dawn

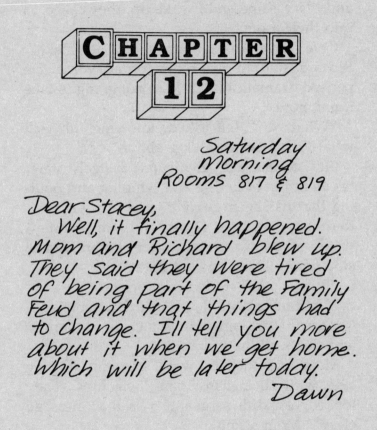

CHAPTER 12

Saturday
Morning
Rooms 817 & 819

Dear Stacey,
   Well, it finally happened.
Mom and Richard blew up.
They said they were tired
of being part of the Family
Feud and that things had
to change. I'll tell you more
about it when we get home.
Which will be later today.
                    Dawn

Mom and Richard had woken up early, eaten breakfast together, and *talked*. When Jeff and Mary Anne and I woke up, they called us into their room.

"We have an announcement to make," Richard said in his most formal voice. He paused dramatically. "We're not going to take it anymore."

"What's *it*?" Jeff asked, knowing full well what Richard was talking about.

"*It*," Mom said, giving Jeff a steely stare, "is all of the bickering and whining and pouting that has been going on. As of right now, that has to change. Dawn and Mary Anne, I want you two to make up. Jeff, I want you to stop acting like a spoiled brat."

"But — " Jeff started to protest.

"No buts about it." Richard cut him off. "You will start behaving in a civilized manner and that's all there is to it."

Mom and Richard were standing side by side with their hands on their hips. They looked like drill sergeants. "Is that message clear?" Mom asked.

"Yes," we muttered. I didn't have to look at Mary Anne to know she was probably about to cry. She hates being yelled at. I guess everyone does.

"Now." Mom let her arms drop to her sides.

"Richard and I have decided that we will spend this last day in Boston together. The three of you said you wanted to see Boston Common and the Public Garden, so that is what we are going to do. But first Richard and I would like to visit the John Hancock Observatory."

Saturday, late morning
The John Hancock Tower
740 ft. off the ground
Dear Claud,
    I'm writing to you from the tallest building in New England. We're so high up that I can see not only all of Boston, but the White Mountains and the Blue Hills in New Hampshire. This is practically the first time the five of us have been together since Thursday. We're trying to be nice. It's not easy.
See you in a few hours.
                    Dawn

After visiting the John Hancock Tower, we strolled up Columbus Avenue to Boston Common. It reminded me a lot of Central Park in New York. It's this huge park area with statues, memorials, and fountains. I saw a band-

109

stand and lots of big old trees and grassy areas for playing Frisbee in.

"Hey, look at that guy," Jeff said, pointing at a man who was wearing a drum, a harmonica, and cymbals.

"He's a one-man band," Richard explained. "Let's give him a dollar and see if he'll play us a tune."

"How about 'The Happy Wanderer'?" Jeff asked. I think he was joking, but no one laughed. We were still feeling a little tense.

We listened to the one-man band play "Hot Time in the Old Town Tonight" (the only song the man knew), and then we visited Frog Pond, which was the site of the first water pumped into the city. But no way would I ever drink it. It was brown and covered in a green slime.

The Public Garden was much more fun.

"Oh, look," Mary Anne cried as we neared the Beacon Street entrance. "It's the ducklings from *Make Way for Ducklings*. Aren't they adorable?"

Mary Anne was talking about the eight bronze ducks from the classic children's story. The book is about the Mallard family and their search for a home through the streets of Boston. Jeff had never heard of it. "It's just a bunch of dumb ducks," he commented as we entered the garden.

110

"Jeff!" Mom said warningly under her breath. "You be nice."

"I want to ride the Swan Boats," Mary Anne said, skipping ahead of us to the pond that sits in the center of the garden.

We followed a tulip-lined path to the water's edge just as one of the boats came into view. It was an old fashioned flat boat with benches on it. In the back, the captain sat behind a beautiful white swan, pedaling the boat like a bicycle.

"It's adorable!" I cried. "Please, Mom! Can we ride it?"

Jeff didn't want to ride, but our parents insisted. He sat sulking on one bench with Mom and Richard while Mary Anne and I sat behind him, smiling stiffly at each other and at the scenery. If we'd been in better moods, it could have been a lot of fun. Mary Anne and I would have been "oohing" and "ahhing" as the captain pedaled us around the pond, under huge weeping willows, and past a beautiful Victorian footbridge.

We bought lunch from a corner deli and ate it on benches near the park. When we'd finished, Richard said, "Well, kids, it's two o'clock. What do you say we get an early start on the trip home?"

Normally, I would have begged to stay longer, but I didn't say a word. Neither did

Mary Anne or Jeff. We walked back to the hotel, climbed in the car, and instantly got into a fight.

"Dawn, move!" Jeff said, tugging on my arm. "I get the window."

"No, you don't," I said, yanking my arm out of his grasp. "You got the window coming here. I get it going back."

Jeff glared at Mary Anne. "Take her window. She can sit in the middle."

I threw my hands up in frustration. "Jeff, don't be a jerk!"

Mary Anne, who had been watching us coolly from her side of the seat, said, "I'll sit in the middle if it means that much to you two."

That made me angry. Mary Anne was acting as if I was being as childish as Jeff. I wasn't.

"No," I shot back. "He's *my* brother. I'll sit in the middle."

I started to move but Jeff grumbled. "Forget it. Just forget it."

Richard, who had been listening to us argue, looked in the rearview mirror and asked, "Are you three quite finished?"

"Yes," I said, slumping down with my head against the window.

"Yes," Mary Anne said, slumping against her window.

"I'm finished," Jeff snapped. "With everything. I want to go back to California tonight."

Mom looked at Richard and sighed. Then she turned around and said, "I'm sorry you feel that way, Jeff, but your plane ticket is for Sunday and that's when you'll leave."

"Maybe we can change it."

"We cannot. Besides, you have to be in the family portrait tomorrow morning."

Suddenly Jeff was all arms and legs. He climbed over our seat and hurled himself into the back of the car. There was barely enough room for him with the luggage and the cooler, but he managed to squeeze himself into a tiny space between two suitcases. That's where he stayed for the entire trip. He didn't talk. He didn't sleep. He just sat there glaring at the rest of us.

Saturday—Homeward bound

Dear Kristy,

This is my final postcard. Mary Anne is sitting next to me, heaving big sighs. Jeff's in the back of the car glaring at everyone. Mom and Richard keep muttering little threats under their breath. And I'm staring out the window, looking for Stoneybrook. What a lousy vacation.

—Dawn

113

"There it is!" Mom cried as we crested the hill by Stoneybrook. "Kids, we're home."

"Thank goodness," I murmured. Our horrible vacation was over. I looked at Mary Anne. Now if only we could end our family feud.

CHAPTER 13

Saterday

Whoa! You wern't kidding when you guys said there were problems at the Baret house.

Claud and I sat for the DeWitts and the Barretts on Saturday and it was war!

It's a good thing Shanon and I read the notbook, because we were prepeared.

We packed our kid-kits and worked out our battle plan in advance.

The kids didn't no what hit them! It was grate!

While Mary Anne and I were in Boston (not speaking to each other and having a terrible time), our BSC associate member, Shannon Kilbourne, filled in for us. It's a good thing, too, because I know Claudia would not have been able to handle the battle at the Barretts' alone.

After the call from Mrs. Barrett at the BSC meeting on Friday, Claud and Shannon made sure they read every entry in the club notebook. Then they put their heads together and came up with a plan to end the fighting between the Barretts and the DeWitts. They put it into action the second Franklin and Mrs. Barrett left.

"All right, guys," Claudia said. "It's a beautiful day. Let's go outside."

Shannon held the door while the seven kids raced onto the front lawn. Not more than two minutes passed before the arguing started.

"Let's play a game," Claudia suggested.

Buddy, who was wearing his cowboy hat, said, "Okay. Let's play Wild West."

Lindsey wrinkled her nose. "I don't like that game, whatever it is. I want to play hopscotch."

"I hate hopscotch," Suzi snapped. "I'm not playing it."

"Well, I'm not playing Wild West with you," Taylor said.

"Who asked you to?" Buddy shot back. Then he stuck out his tongue.

Claudia and Shannon looked at each other and nodded.

"Buddy, Suzi, and Marnie," Claudia shouted. "Come with me. We're going into the backyard."

"What about us?" Taylor asked, confused.

"You're staying with me," Shannon replied.

"Good." Claudia pretended to be on the Barretts' side. "We'll play by ourselves."

The Barrett kids turned up their noses at the DeWitts and followed Claudia around the side of the house. When they reached the backyard, Claud said, "Okay, you guys. How about a game of Red Light, Green Light?"

"Okay," Suzi said. "You be it."

Claud stood at one end of the yard with her back turned and Buddy, Suzi, and Marnie lined up at the other.

"Green light," Claud said.

The three kids raced forward. (Buddy took Marnie's hand, since she's too little to understand the game.)

"Red light." Claud spun around and said, "I saw Marnie, Buddy, and Suzi."

"But that's all of us," Buddy protested.

"I know," Claud said. "But there are so few of you, it was easy to spot who was moving."

Suzi folded her arms across her chest. "Let's play a different game. How about Mother, May I?"

"All right," Claud said. "Why don't you be the mother?"

Mother, May I? lasted about five minutes before the kids grew bored.

"These games would be a lot more fun if we had more people," Buddy said, slumping down on the grass.

Claud sat next to him. "I know where we could find more people."

"Where?" Suzi asked.

"In the front yard with Shannon. The DeWitt kids."

Buddy leapt to his feet. "Let's go get them."

Claud shook her head sadly. "You always fight with Lindsey and the others. No, I think we better just play by ourselves."

"Please?" Suzi said, jumping up and down. "Couldn't we call them?"

"I don't know," Claud said slowly.

"We won't fight." Buddy held up two fingers. "Scout's honor."

"Pretty please," Suzi added. "With a cherry on top?"

Claud nearly burst out laughing, but she bit her lip and kept a very serious face. "Well, if you think you can get along . . ."

"We can! We can!" Buddy and Suzi cried.

"Then we'll give it a try."

In the front yard, Shannon was having the same discussion with the DeWitt kids. They'd tried playing Red Rover, Red Rover but it didn't work very well with four children. Then they'd tried A Tisket, A Tasket but that quickly fizzled, too. Soon the DeWitts were begging to play with the Barretts.

Claud and Shannon met at the corner of the house like generals planning a battlefield truce. They spoke in loud voices so the kids could hear them.

"Buddy and the others swear they won't fight," Claudia said loudly. "They said they like the DeWitt kids."

"Well," Shannon replied, "the DeWitts like the Barretts. They want to invite them to play a game of Red Rover. Would the Barretts be able to play nicely?"

Claud snuck a glance over her shoulder at the three kids huddled behind her. They nodded briskly. "They'll try," Claud said to Shannon.

Shannon stuck out her hand. "Let's shake on it."

"Yea!" The kids greeted each other like long lost friends.

For the next two hours, they played every

outdoor game that Claudia and Shannon knew. And a couple that hadn't been invented. Finally they collapsed, exhausted, on the grass. Before long, Lindsey began to giggle.

"What is it?" Buddy asked. "What's the joke?"

"The joke is, I can't remember why we were fighting," Lindsey said, continuing to giggle. "Can you?"

Buddy sat up, and squeezed his eyes shut, trying to think. "Well, that trip to the petting zoo was kind of a disaster."

Lindsey nodded. "That's 'cause our parents wanted us to like each other so much."

"So everything went wrong," Taylor added.

"Then Mom started acting weird," Buddy said.

Suzi agreed. "Not like our real mom at all."

"Like some TV mom," Buddy said. "Trying to cook and clean and be perfect."

"Dad's been weird, too," Taylor said. "Really tense."

Lindsey flopped back on the grass. "I think we should tell our parents to cool it."

"Yeah," Buddy said, sitting down beside Lindsey. "They should just relax and be themselves."

Claud and Shannon hoped the kids didn't notice, but they were both beaming. They'd

120

helped put an end to the battle of the DeWitts vs. the Barretts. And they'd learned a lesson. As Shannon put it: "People shouldn't try to be something they aren't. It just messes things up."

When Franklin and Mrs. Barrett pulled into the driveway half an hour later, they were greeted by seven grim faces.

"Oh, no," Mrs. Barrett muttered as she leapt out of the car and hurried to the children. "Kids? Is anything the matter?"

"Yes!" they shouted.

"Okay," Franklin said with a resigned sigh. "What is it?"

"We're hungry," Buddy said with a huge grin. Then to Franklin and Mrs. Barrett's surprise, he draped one arm over Lindsey's shoulder and asked, "What's for dinner?"

Franklin and Mrs. Barrett turned to each other, amazed. But before they could say a single word, they were surrounded by seven happy, giggling kids.

CHAPTER 14

Ding-dong!

At eleven on the dot on Sunday morning, the photographer arrived at our house. Jeff was sitting in the living room wearing his torn jeans, striped T-shirt (with a jam stain on the sleeve), and his baseball cap. I was in the kitchen, dressed in a jean skirt, red cotton T-shirt, and blue chamois shirt knotted at the waist. (After the terrible four days I had just spent with Mary Anne, I wasn't about to wear any outfit that matched hers.)

"Oh, my goodness!" Mom cried from upstairs. "Marshall Gaines is here. Kids! Kids, where are you?"

"Jeff and I are downstairs," I shouted back.

"I'm glad you're ready," Mom said as she hurried down the stairs. She was wearing her blue silk dress that shows off her eyes, and her pearl earrings and necklace. "These photographers charge by the hour. One minute over and it can get very pricey. AAAAAAUGH!"

Mom's scream was loud enough to bring Richard to the top of the stairs. "What's the matter, Sharon?" he called. "Are you all right?"

"The kids." She pointed at Jeff and me. "They're not dressed. The photographer is here and they're not — "

"We're dressed," I said calmly. "We just decided to go casual."

"Up the stairs!" Mom ordered. "Both of you. Into your good clothes. Now."

Mom rarely gets angry, but when she does, her face turns bright red. Today, it looked like a tomato. That's why Jeff and I did exactly what she told us to do.

Ding-dong!

"Isn't anyone going to answer the door?" Mom asked in exasperation.

"I thought you answered it," Richard snapped as he hurried down the stairs. The strain of the past week was showing on his face. "What's going on around here?"

Mary Anne passed Jeff and me on the stairs. She was wearing an old pair of jeans and a sweat shirt.

"Should we tell Mary Anne how mad Mom's going to be when she sees her outfit?" Jeff whispered.

I shook my head. "No, let her find out herself."

Jeff and I waited to see what would happen. We didn't have to wait long before we heard shouting. This time it was coming from Mom *and* Richard. A very red-faced Mary Anne hurried back up the stairs.

"Something wrong, Mary Anne?" I asked sweetly.

She answered me by slamming her bedroom door in my face. Jeff and I smiled at each other.

"You kids have five minutes to change and get back down here!" Mom shouted from below. Jeff and I raced to our rooms.

I decided to wear the outfit Mary Anne and I had chosen the week before. It was hanging on the closet door and I'd already picked out my jewelry and shoes. Jeff had brought only one nice outfit to Connecticut. A pair of tan slacks and a sweater.

When we reappeared downstairs we walked headlong into an argument between Mom and Richard, and the photographer.

"I think the portrait should be taken in the yard," Marshall Gaines was saying. "That big tree provides the perfect backdrop."

"I really want to pose on the front porch," Mom said stubbornly. "I've always wanted the front porch."

"Why does it have to be outside?" Richard

cut in. "Why can't we have a formal photo in the living room in front of the fireplace?"

"Oh, Richard." Mom rolled her eyes. "That's so dull."

"Dull? Dull?" Richard sputtered. "I say it's elegant. Much better than a family of hillbillies on the porch."

"Hillbillies?" Mom repeated huffily. "Now that's a nice thing to say!"

"I've got it!" Jeff cried. "We'll take it in the barn. We can each get in a stall and pretend to be an animal." Jeff dropped to his knees and crawled in a circle around the room. "Mooooo! Mooooo! Mooooo!"

"Stop that mooing." Richard put his hands to his temples. "How can anyone think?"

"Excuse me!" Marshall Gaines interrupted. "Would you like me to come back another day?"

"Yes!" Jeff shouted.

"Jeff, hush up," Mom ordered. "We have to take this photo today." She turned to the photographer and tried to remain calm. "As soon as Mary Anne comes downstairs, we'll take the picture."

"We still haven't decided where we should pose," Richard pointed out.

"Pose in the kitchen," Mom said, throwing her arms in the air. "I don't care. Just take the picture."

"I've got an idea," Marshall Gaines said. "We'll pose in the living room first and then take a shot on the porch. How does that sound?"

"Fine!" Richard marched into the living room. By this time Mary Anne had come back downstairs. She was wearing the dress we'd picked out.

"We're posing inside?" she asked.

"Yes!" everyone, including the photographer, answered her.

Mary Anne's eyes widened. "You don't have to shout."

It took several minutes for Marshall Gaines to position everyone because no one wanted to get too close to anyone else. He finally decided to seat Mary Anne and Jeff and me on the couch, with Mom and Richard standing behind it.

"I'll take a few Polaroids of this pose," Marshall Gaines said. "Then we can decide if we want to continue with it."

He set up his tripod and was ready to take the first photo when Mary Anne suddenly bolted off the couch and ran for the kitchen. "Wait a minute. We forgot someone!" she yelled.

"Who?" I asked, taking a head count. There were five of us. "No one's missing."

Mary Anne returned, cuddling Tigger.

"Poor baby. We almost forgot you."

"Oh, no, you don't," Mom said, stepping in front of the couch. "I will not have animals in this portrait."

"But Tigger's part of the family," Mary Anne protested.

"He is *not* part of the family," Mom said stiffly. "He's just a cat."

"Dad," Mary Anne looked up at Richard with tears in her eyes. "Please?"

Richard turned to Mom. "I don't see the harm in having Tigger in the picture. Come on, Sharon, let her hold him."

Mom's voice was tense. "Okay. Fine."

Mary Anne sat down on the couch and just as Marshall Gaines was about to shoot the photo, Tigger sprang off her lap. She started to go after him, but Richard put his hand on her shoulder. "Let him go, Mary Anne."

"Take the picture," Mom said with a frozen smile on her face. "Please! Before we completely disintegrate."

Mr. Gaines posed us in different positions, trying to make us look like one big happy family. We didn't. After about fifteen minutes, he handed me and Mary Anne the Polaroids.

"Here, girls," Marshall Gaines said. "Take a look at these and tell me what you think."

He handed me the first shot. I was glaring at Mary Anne. Mary Anne was leaning as far away from Jeff as she could get. Jeff had crossed his eyes as he stared at the camera. Mom and Richard were smiling with clenched teeth.

Mary Anne and I burst out laughing.

"We look terrible!" I exclaimed.

Mary Anne was giggling so hard that tears rolled down her cheeks. "This is possibly the worst family portrait in history."

Jeff, Mom, and Richard joined in our laughter as we examined photo after photo of ourselves with cross faces, jerking away from each other, looking miserable.

After we stopped laughing, Mom dashed upstairs to repair her mascara, which had run in two streaks down her cheeks from laughing so hard. While she was gone, Jeff and Richard chatted with the photographer about his equipment and I helped Mary Anne find Tigger.

As we headed back to the living room, I caught Mary Anne's arm. "Mary Anne," I whispered. "I feel pretty silly."

She nodded. "I don't know what happened to us."

"I'm really sorry for everything," I said.

"Me, too."

Then we hugged each other.

The rest of the photo session went smoothly. We posed in front of the fireplace for Richard and on the porch for Mom. We even took a couple of shots by the big maple tree for Marshall. By the time he finished, we agreed we'd had a lot of fun.

Unfortunately, the end of the photo session meant that it was time for Jeff to pack. In just half an hour we would have to leave for the airport.

We all trooped upstairs to Jeff's room. Mary Anne and I stretched out on his bed. Richard perched on the edge of Jeff's desk and Mom helped him pack.

"I wish we hadn't fought so much while you were here," I said as I watched Jeff put his striped T-shirt, which really was too small for him, into his suitcase.

"Yeah." Jeff scratched his head. "I can't even remember how it all began."

"Well," said Mary Anne, her hands clasped in her lap, "I may have been too sensitive, but I got upset because I thought Jeff was hurting Dad's feelings."

"Really?" Jeff asked. "How?"

"Well, you didn't like the museums and you made fun of him because he can't throw a softball."

"It's true," Richard cut in. "I can't throw a softball. Or catch one. In fact, sports are not my thing at all. But I wanted to spend time with Jeff."

I turned to Mary Anne. "At first I got mad at you because I thought you were criticizing Jeff too much. But then Jeff really did start acting like a spoiled brat. So I got mad at him."

"So this whole fight was *my* fault," Jeff exclaimed. "I started everything."

"No," I said. "If it was all your fault, nobody else would have been fighting."

Jeff kicked at the carpet with the toe of his sneaker. "I know I acted like a jerk. It's just that nothing was like what I thought it'd be." He raised his head and looked at Mom and me. "When it was just the three of us, things were different."

"That's something you're going to have to live with," Mom said, draping her arm over his shoulder. "Richard and Mary Anne are part of our lives now."

"It's not just our family," Jeff said. "It's everything. My friends here found new friends and completely forgot about me."

"That's not true," Mary Anne replied. "The triplets ask about you every time I baby-sit for them."

"Really?" Jeff's face brightened.

Mary Anne nodded. "Honest."

"Look," Mom opened her arms. "What do you say, we all hug each other and then enjoy our last few moments together."

Jeff and I stepped into Mom's embrace. Then

130

Richard and Mary Anne wrapped their arms around us. I breathed a huge sigh of relief. Our family feud had ended.

Ding-dong!

"Now who could that be?" Mom asked as we carried Jeff's bags down the stairs.

"Probably the photographer saying he found the perfect location for our portrait," I said.

"Yeah," Jeff chuckled. "And for only a million dollars more, he'll actually take the picture."

Mary Anne answered the door. "Oh, Jeff!" she called. "Your friends are here."

"What friends?" Jeff asked, adjusting his baseball cap on his head.

"Us!" Byron, Adam, and Jordan popped their heads inside the doorway. "We came to say good-bye."

Jeff's face lit up with a grin that seemed to stretch from ear to ear. "Hey, you guys want to see my souvenirs from Boston?"

"Sure!"

As the triplets stepped into the front hall, Mary Anne and I exchanged smiles. Things were back to normal.

CHAPTER 15

*"California, here I come,
Right back where I started from."*

It was Richard's idea to sing every song ever written about California as we drove to the airport. Richard, Jeff, and the Pike triplets (who had called their mom and gotten permission to come with us) were having a blast singing at the top of their lungs. Mary Anne and I just covered our ears and laughed. It was great to see Jeff and Richard have fun together.

At the airport, we unloaded Jeff's bags and while Richard parked the car, the rest of us walked Jeff to the loading gate. When we reached the waiting area, Jeff and the triplets made a beeline for the hospitality table. Within seconds, they'd jammed their pockets with packets of smoked almonds, little white .

creamer cartons, and red and white plastic stir straws.

"All right, guys," Mom said, guiding them away from the table. "That's enough souvenirs for now."

"Hey, Jeff!" Byron said. "When you get on the plane, get me a barf bag, will you?"

"Sure!" Jeff said. "Anything else?"

"I'd like one of those cool oxygen masks that drop out of the ceiling," Adam said.

"Those are only for emergencies," Jordan said to his brother. "Jeff can't get that."

"Want to bet?" Adam said, folding his arms across his chest. "Jeff can do anything."

Jeff beamed proudly at his friends. "I'll talk to the flight attendant and see what I can do."

Richard joined us and, almost immediately, a voice came over the speaker. "May I have your attention, please? Flight four-one-seven is now ready to board."

"Oh, no," I groaned. "That's your plane. It's time for you to go!"

Mom handed Jeff his ticket and boarding pass. Then she gave him her usual list of last minute instructions. "Be sure and eat right, take plenty of vitamins, work hard in school, be careful on your bike, listen to your father, call me once a week, and — "

Jeff and I finished her sentence for her.

"Write me. You never write," we said, imitating her voice and shaking our finger at her.

Mom's eyes widened. "Do I always say that?"

Jeff and I looked at each other and then back at Mom. "Always."

"Well, it's because you *don't* write," Mom said, straightening the collar on Jeff's shirt and smoothing his hair. "I think I've gotten one letter from you in the past six months."

"I'll write, Mom," Jeff said, kissing her on the cheek. "I promise."

Mom's eyes teared up and her chin quivered a little as she hugged and kissed him. "Good. Because I'm going to miss you."

Then we wrapped our arms around Jeff. Mary Anne and Richard and me. "I'm going to miss you, too," Mary Anne said. "And I'm really glad we're all friends again."

"Yeah, I just wish it could have happened a little earlier," I said.

"Jeff'll just have to come back for another visit soon," Richard said.

"Okay," Jeff replied. Then he grinned mischievously. "Hey! I've got an idea. Why don't we take a trip to Boston?"

"Great idea!" I giggled. "I'd love to see what it looks like when I'm not angry."

Several weeks after Jeff left, a package arrived in the mail from the photographer, Marshall Gaines. It was the proofs from our photo session. We waited until we'd eaten dinner before we sat down and looked at them.

"Oh, these are very nice," Mom said, flipping through the pictures. "It's going to be difficult to choose just one."

Richard nodded in approval. "I have to say it, we are a good-looking family."

"Not all the time." I held up the proofs from the beginning of the photo session. "Take a look at these."

"It's amazing," Mom said, chuckling. "Every single one of us looks angry."

"Even Tigger," Mary Anne said, pointing to the shot where Tigger was leaping off her lap.

We took turns holding up first the funny shots, then the good shots, and laughing.

"I think we should have this one blown up and framed," I said, holding up an angry photo. "To show us how silly we were to let things get so out of hand. And as a reminder never to let it happen again."

"That's a great idea, Dawn!" Mom exclaimed.

"But we should also frame one of the happy shots," Mary Anne added. "To show us how great we can look when we get along."

And that's what we did. Now two family portraits hang on our living room wall, each in a lovely frame. One's funny, and the other's beautiful. We put them together so we'd never forget our family feud.

About the Author

ANN M. MARTIN did *a lot* of baby-sitting when she was growing up in Princeton, New Jersey. Now her favorite baby-sitting charge is her cat, Mouse, who lives with her in her Manhattan apartment.

Ann Martin's Apple Paperbacks include *Yours Turly, Shirley; Ten Kids, No Pets; With You and Without You; Bummer Summer;* and all the other books in the Baby-sitters Club series.

She is a former editor of books for children, and was graduated from Smith College. She likes ice cream, the beach, and *I Love Lucy;* and she hates to cook.

Look for #65

STACEY'S BIG CRUSH

When I walked into math class the next day, Tom Cruise was in the room.

I don't know how he got there. I don't know what he was doing. I don't know how long he was going to stay.

But here's what I did know: My knees were weak. There was not enough air in the room. And I was not dreaming.

There I was, Stacey McGill, native New Yorker. I was used to celebrities on the streets of NYC. I could pass them by with just a casual glance.

But this was different. As I walked to my seat, I could not feel my feet touch the ground.

My brain? Total mush. I'd start to put a thought together, then HE would smile at something. Dimples would crease his cheeks, and I'd be gone. Lost. His slate blue eyes would flash across the room, and it was nuclear meltdown time. Then he'd run his hand through his wavy, light brown hair, and I was afraid they would have to scrape me off the floor.

Do I sound like I was in *love*? I was. But somewhere, deep in the back of my pea-soupy brain, some little germs of reality were coming together. This was not really Tom Cruise. Tom Cruise would not be in a math class at Stoney-brook Middle School. He would not be fiddling with a piece of chalk, talking to Mr. Z., glancing down at a sheet on the desk.

That didn't matter, though. It didn't change the way he looked, or the effect he was having on me.

But it didn't sink in who it *really* was, until Mr. Z. turned to the class and spoke.

"Okay, everybody," he said, just after the bell rang. "I'm pleased to introduce your new teacher, Mr. Ellenburg."

My heart stopped.

This was Wesley Ellenburg.

I had to let that idea sink in. I felt like an idiot for not having realized it right away. But I had an excuse. I had taken temporary leave of my senses.

Read all the latest books
in the Baby-sitters Club series
by Ann M. Martin

142

by Ann M. Martin

More titles... ▶

The Baby-sitters Club titles continued...

Available wherever you buy books...or use this order form.

Scholastic Inc., P.O. Box 7502, 2931 E. McCarty Street, Jefferson City, MO 65102

Please send me the books I have checked above. I am enclosing $_____
(please add $2.00 to cover shipping and handling). Send check or money order - no
cash or C.O.D.s please.

Name _____

Address _____

City_____ State/Zip_____

Tell us your birth date! _____

BSC792

What's the next-best thing to meeting Ann M. Martin in person?

Having her exclusive life story!

Ann M. Martin
The Story of the Author of

Find out what Ann was like when she was a teenager and read about her life as a famous author! This so-cool biography is filled with private photographs and personal messages from Ann. After reading it, you'll know all there is to know about your favorite author!

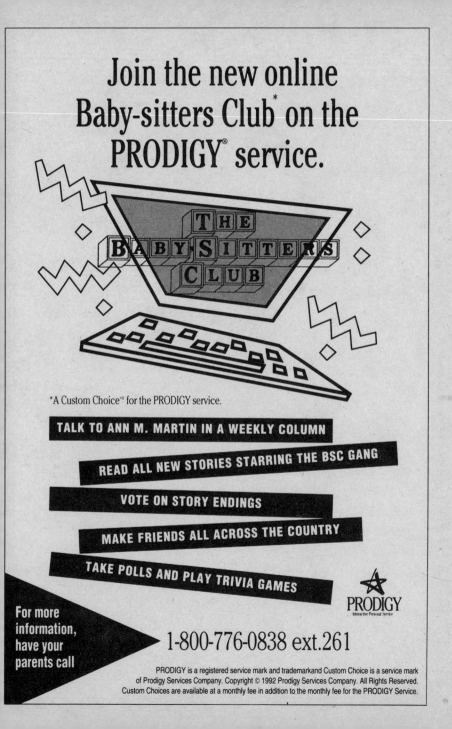